THE TRACKERS

RAY HOGAN

THORNDIKE
CHIVERS

This Large Print edition is published by Thorndike Press, Waterville, Maine, USA and by AudioGO Ltd, Bath, England.
Thorndike Press, a part of Gale, Cengage Learning.
The text of this Large Print edition is unabridged.
Other aspects of the book may vary from the original edition.
Set in 16 pt. Plantin.

LIBRARY OF CONGRESS CATALOGING-IN-PUBLICATION DATA

Hogan, Ray, 1908–1998.
The trackers / by Ray Hogan.
p. cm. — (Thorndike Press large print western)
ISBN-13: 978-1-4104-2615-4
ISBN-10: 1-4104-2615-7
1. Large type books. I. Title.
PS3558.O3473T7 2010
813'.54—dc22   2010007690

BRITISH LIBRARY CATALOGUING-IN-PUBLICATION DATA AVAILABLE

Published in 2010 in the U.S. by arrangement with Golden West Literary Agency.
Published in 2010 in the U.K. by arrangement with Golden West Literary Agency.

U.K. Hardcover: 978 1 408 49152 2 (Chivers Large Print)
U.K. Softcover: 978 1 408 49153 9 (Camden Large Print)

Printed and bound in Great Britain by
CPI Antony Rowe, Chippenham, Wiltshire.

1 2 3 4 5 6 7 14 13 12 11 10

THE TRACKERS

1

He was an unruly man and no stranger to trouble. Alone, he sat at a table near the streaky glass window of the Bon Ton Café and stared out onto the deserted street, shriveling in the summer's murderous heat. Elsewhere in the stifling square of room that served as Harmony's only restaurant, the cook rattled dishes, clattered pots and pans, and went about his work.

Those were the normal, the everyday, the usual things, but beneath them, like a sullen, quiet-flowing underground stream, Matt Campion sensed the unexpected. The *feel* of trouble was there; the same deadly, breathless tension he had experienced in a half a hundred other towns during the years that were the past. And just as he had been then, he was ready now, for, if time had taught him anything, it had taught him that the answer to violence was greater violence.

And then quite suddenly the stern, harsh

corners of his wind-burned face relaxed. The fingers of his hands that gripped the edge of the scarred table eased off. He was a damned fool — but old habits were hard to break. Harmony's troubles, whatever they might be, could in no way touch him. He was a pilgrim, en route to a new life, a new destination; a stranger in a fresh land leaving the turbulence of the old ways far behind. In Harmony he simply paused; sought only food for his belly, a bed for his saddle-weary frame. Then he would again be on his way.

It had been a long trail from the old family home on the Missouri-Kansas borders, one that would tot up to several thousand meandering, often danger-filled miles. But he did not regret the years and the aimless drifting. In the beginning there had been no choice. When the war was over there was nothing left of the farm his parents had willed him. The destructive triumvirate of Union Army Order Number Eleven, the Kansas Jayhawkers, and the Missouri Guerrillas had combined to reduce everything to worthless shambles. He had taken one look at the graying ashes, the lifeless fields, and ridden on.

In the years that followed he had wandered back and forth across the Territories of the vast West, working at odd jobs when they were to be found, gambling in the trail towns when he had the money, never thinking too much about the future. Trouble was an all-too-constant companion and the worn, cedar-handled six-gun at his hip became the only thing in which he placed his faith.

It was a pointless but tempering sort of existence for Matt Campion at the outset, and for a long time it pleased and satisfied him. But the day came eventually when he felt the need to halt, to find a place to his liking, put down his roots and forget the way of violence and the gun hanging at his side.

That, too, was long in coming, but come it did. In Wichita at the end of a cattle drive, his luck at a faro table ran wild. He won, hand over fist, and when he walked away at last he had better than a thousand dollars in his pockets. His good fortune did not end there. That same night he heard of a small ranch that could be bought outright; a place deep in the lush Cloverdale area of New Mexico Territory. It was not far from the Arizona line, only a few miles from the Mexican border.

The price was low. Cattle could be obtained from Mexican ranchers for practically nothing — at no cost at all if a man would get out and work the brakes. There was always a good market for beef at the Indian agencies, where there was a constant need for meat to keep the government's sulky wards in hand. That next day he was on the trail, headed west. Now, weeks later, he was deep in the broad, stark beauty of New Mexico, but still a long ride from his goal.

He stirred impatiently on the hard-backed chair and wished he had a smoke. He had run out of the makings, must remember to buy a supply when he finished eating. From where he sat he could look down the street and sea the stable where he had taken his horse. The big sorrel had been about done in when they reached Harmony; those last two days had been rough going and hot. But the red was getting the care he needed now — and he wasn't having to wait for his evening meal.

Campion glanced toward the partition near the back of the room. Behind it the cook rattled dishes and pans busily. The noise was almost superfluous, as though the aproned owner of the café wished Matt to know he was still there, was working to prepare the food.

"Hey, cook — how about that grub?"

"Keep your shirt on, mister. I'm movin' fast as I can."

Campion shifted restlessly on his chair, allowed his gaze to swing to the only other customers in the restaurant: a middle-aged merchant and a plump woman at a table across the room. The man wore a gray suit, white shirt, and high, starched collar with a carefully knotted bow tie. The woman had a maroon-colored silk dress that supported a large amount of heavy lace. Both were somewhat overdressed, considering the heat. They were celebrating, Matt decided: probably a birthday or perhaps an anniversary.

He watched them idly. They ate with a quiet, furious intensity, as though something hurried them, pushed them to complete the chore and have done with it. Somewhere in the room a trapped fly buzzed noisily. The man paused, cast a furtive glance at Campion with small, bright eyes, then looked away quickly.

The cook appeared in the doorway of the partition. He paused, the platter of steak, potatoes, biscuits and gravy Campion had ordered in his hands. He touched the couple briefly with his look and came forward. Halting before Matt he placed the food on the table.

11

"More coffee?" he asked, his ruddy face expressionless.

Campion nodded, picked up his knife and fork. He heard the merchant and his wife shove back their chairs, get to their feet. There was the faint chink of silver as the man dropped several coins on the table to cover the check.

The cook refilled Campion's cup from a small, granite pot, spilling a little of the black, steaming liquid as he did. He said nothing to the departing guests, extended no thanks, no farewell. It came to Matt Campion at that moment that the pair had concluded their meal and left abruptly the instant his own serving was made. Once again he had that vague feeling of impending danger.

"Nothin' else?"

Campion lifted his eyes to the cook, studied him thoughtfully for the length of a deep breath. "This'll do for now," he said finally, and looked down. "Might be wanting some pie later — and leave that pot here where I can get at it."

The man bobbed his bald head, shuffled off toward the partition. Matt began to eat, taking to the food with the relish of a healthy man too many days on the trail and heartily sick of his own cooking.

12

Movement in the street caught the tail of Matt's eye. Two men crossed in front of the window, walking so fast he had only a fleeting glimpse of them. Harmony was at last coming to life. But it was not unusual for people to remain indoors during the heat of the day, he knew. The sun was a potent factor in the high, western country.

He began to feel better. The meat was tender, the potatoes crisp-fried, and the gravy to his liking. Coffee could be a bit stronger but he was in no mood to quibble. It was good to just sit at a table, to eat well, to hear voices and see human beings again. The endless, empty miles could be terribly lonely at times. When he finished with his meal, he'd drop by a saloon, have a drink or two. He might even sit in on a few hands of cards, ask some casual questions and find out what was chewing at the town. He was tired, but another couple of hours' conversation would be right nice. A man got hungry for other things besides food.

More persons moved by the window. A group of four or five men this time. All appeared headed in the same direction and he wondered, speculating on what the attraction might be. He paused in his eating, stared out onto the street, conscious of something odd. It came to him a moment later: there were no women in sight. He frowned, sipped slowly at his coffee.

He heard the screen door at the front of the café open. It pulled back, hung, did not close. He listened to the dry rasp of boot heels scuffing on the sill. It was a careful sound, intentionally muted.

The hard pressure of danger was upon him once more, now tightening his nerves, tensing his long body. He laid his knife and fork down, moving gently and purposefully. He rested his hands on the edge of the table, considered what he should do: get up fast, lunge to one side and draw. The problem and its solution came to him at once. He had been through it many times, and experience was a skilled teacher in a school where only the adept pupils stayed alive.

But that was all wrong!

That was the old way of life — and he was pointing for the new. He was too suspicious. He had lived with trouble so long that he saw it in every sound, every unfamiliar movement. He was a stranger here in Harmony, he had nothing to fear — and he would look plenty foolish if he came boiling around with a pistol in his hand and discovered whoever had entered the café had simply come in for a meal. There was no —

His reasoning came to a sudden, jolting

14

stop. The cook had stepped from behind his partition. He held a double barreled shotgun. The tall, rabbit-ear hammers were drawn to full-cock position. The twin, black holes in the muzzle looked large as silver dollars.

Matt stared at the man, more startled than afraid. "What the hell —"

From behind a voice said, "Get up easy, mister. Slow like. Leave your hands flat on the table."

Campion did not move. A deep fury was running through him suddenly. He should have heeded his inner warnings, listened to the intuition that so many times had proved unerring. He swore softly under his breath. It was too late now. How many men stood back of him he could not tell — but it did not matter. There was no arguing with the cook and his shotgun.

He rose slowly, a tall man well over six feet and all muscled out to near two hundred pounds. Reaching his full height he hung there, poised, slightly crouched like a gray-eyed wolf at bay, trapped but not necessarily caught.

"Raise your hands now — up high. And turn around." It was the same voice.

Matt Campion wheeled deliberately, lifting his arms as he did. He faced the speaker,

15

a squat, blond man with a star pinned to his pocket of his black sateen shirt. Beyond him stood three more men, one a slim Mexican who also wore a badge. A whiteness began to show along the edge of Campion's jaw. Time and events had bred little love in his heart for lawmen. He was again getting a taste of how the representatives of authority worked.

"What's this?" he demanded bluntly.

The lawman's mouth was grim. "Don't act cute with me. Get his gun, Juan."

The Mexican moved forward, circled Matt carefully, and came in from behind. Campion felt an abrupt lightness at his hip as the weapon was jerked from its holster.

"I'm asking you again, Marshal — what's this all about?"

The lawman shook his head angrily. "Don't be callin' me the marshal! You know damn well I'm the deputy. And if you want it all spelled out for you, I'm takin' you in for murder. For two murders, in fact, and a little robbery on the side!"

2

For a time there was absolute silence in the heat-laden, tension-loaded room. The fly buzzed suddenly again, angrily, loudly. Campion heard the cook step back, heard the metallic click of dry springs as he released the shotgun's hammers, the dull thump as he stood it against the wall.

Campion's long lips pulled into a hard, down-curving line. "You're way off the trail, Deputy. Just rode into your town. I don't know anything about a murder or a robbery."

"Figured you'd be sayin' that," the lawman replied. "Didn't think you'd be admittin' it — leastwise, not at the start."

The implication was plain. Matt said, "Meaning I will later?"

"We got a witness," the lawman said with satisfaction. "Reckon that's all it will take to put a rope around your neck. Somebody go after Jud?"

"He's comin'," one of the men answered. "Told him to meet us at the jail."

Campion felt the walls of the hot, stifling room closing in about him. Again he cursed himself silently for his own carelessness. The corners of his face settled into sharp angles and a hardness tempered the surface of his eyes. Trouble had a way of searching out a man, finding him, but Matt Campion had the answer to it: violence. He studied the men before him. The Mexican was the nearest, little more than a stride away. And the shotgun was no longer at his back.

"A witness!" he snarled. "You haven't got yourself a witness — you've got a man who's a liar or else is making a mistake. Nobody saw me kill anybody for one big reason — I haven't!"

"Maybe," the deputy said indifferently. "Come on, we're goin' over to the jailhouse."

Campion did not stir. He was considering his best move, calculating his chances. One quick lunge, grab the Mexican and whirl him around as a shield. He would have a gun then — two if he wished: his and the one the dark-faced little lawman was holding in his hand. But that first move, in the face of four ready pistols — it would have to be sudden, take them off guard. . . .

18

"You're not railroading me, Deputy," he said, stalling for time, for the right moment. "This is a trumped-up deal and I'm not taking —"

"Maybe you'd like to try resistin' arrest?" the lawman suggested mildly. "Won't make no difference to me. Or to the town. Henry Toon was mighty well thought of around these parts."

"Henry Toon?"

"The marshal — one of the men you shot. Or maybe, bein' a stranger, you didn't know his name. Other man was Ed Wilson, the bank clerk. He's the one you took the money off. He's got friends, too."

"And you're claiming I killed them both?"

"I'm knowin' it — and you took forty-five hundred dollars' payroll they was packin' out to the Little Wonder Mine."

"You're plumb crazy," Campion said in thick disgust. "Never heard of them, or saw them either. Today, yesterday or any other time. You're trying to slap a brand on the wrong steer."

"Reckon we'll see," the deputy murmured. "Get to movin'. We're goin' over to the jailhouse."

"Maybe we ought to search him for the money, Willis," one of the men suggested. "Jud said weren't nothin' in his gear. Must still have it on him."

The pattern of things was beginning to shape up in Matt Campion's mind; the hurried eating of the couple unexpectedly caught at the scene of promised trouble; the delay that had occurred in the preparing of his meal to permit the examination of his gear and the assembling of sufficient guns to handle the crisis. . . . The quiet, hushed town, the deserted, lifeless street.

The deputy twitched his shoulders. "All right, go ahead and have your look. You do it, Juan. Rest of you spread out some, get in a circle. This'n looks like a real curly wolf to me."

Campion saw the Mexican hand his guns to one of the men near him and then move in close. The deputy and the others, cautious and watchful, tightened their guard.

He said: "Tell you right now what you'll find; a little over a thousand dollars. Money I brought along to buy myself a ranch with."

He felt the Mexican's quick hands race over him, locate the money belt that encircled his waist. The little deputy handed it to his fellow lawman.

"It is fat with many bills and coins. I think there is much money there."

"Keep your guns on him while I look."

Matt watched the deputy thumb through

the sheaf of currency and count the few gold coins. He had hesitated to carry so large a sum on his person but there had been no other answer. No one had known much about the southwestern corner of New Mexico Territory into which he proposed to travel, and the banker in Wichita whom he had approached with the idea of obtaining a draft had discouraged the thought. He wasn't certain there was a bank yet in that part of the country and, without one, he had said, a draft was no more than a piece of paper.

"About an even thousand," the deputy announced. "Leaves around thirty-five hundred missin'. You sure there ain't no more, Juan?"

"There is no more," the Mexican said, shrugging.

"How about inside his boots?" the cook offered.

The deputy thought for a moment. "No use wastin' time here. We get him over to the jailhouse, we'll strip him down to hide. Doubt if we find anythin', however. My guess is he hid the rest somewhere, just in case he got tripped up."

"That money's mine," Campion stated, his words sharp and clear. "Won it at a faro table in Wichita. I can prove it if you give me a chance."

"Reckon a man can prove anythin' he wants if he has the right kind of friends," the deputy observed drily. "I'll ask you once more, mister — you comin' along peaceful or do I lay this gun barrel acrosst your head?"

Anger flared through Campion. Hot, promising words surged to his lips — and died. His shoulders moved in a slight gesture of resignation. There was an answer to this somewhere; no point in getting riled over it, especially with the odds stacked wrong against him. There would be a way out, there had to be. That witness the deputy had spoken of: once he got a close look he would realize he was wrong.

Besides, he wanted it all cleared up with no echoing ill will to haunt him down through the years. This country was to be his new home. Some of these men likely could become his friends; there was a good chance he would be doing business in the town. Best he go along with the law, set things straight.

"All right," he said. "I've got nothing to be shying away from."

One of the men behind the deputy laughed shortly. "He says he's got nothin' to shy from! Don't mind tellin' all of you

22

I'd be mighty skittish was I the man who'd buckwhacked Henry Toon!"

The remark apparently had hidden meaning but it was lost on Campion. He gave the man a dry smile, said, "Not being guilty, I'm not," and walked toward the door.

He felt the hard, thrusting pressure of two gun barrels jam into his spine as he stepped into the street. A considerable crowd had gathered and was standing in the broad, lingering heat. A shout went up immediately. The gathering surged forward and from somewhere in its depths a voice cried: "What you goin' to do with him, Willis?"

The deputy paused. "Watch him," he murmured to the Mexican and pushed out in front.

Willis Biderbeck was a small man, small in stature, small in mind. All his life he had been in secondary positions and now, finally, he was the one in command. He held up his hands, palms outward, for silence.

"I've got the man," he said. "No doubt in my mind he's the one who done it. But we're a law abidin' town and I aim to see he gets a fair trial, same as anywhere else in the Territory. Judge'll be here tomorrow and he'll take over."

"Waste of time," another voice declared. "If you're so all fired sure he's the killer,

23

let's do the job right now!"

"String him up!"

"Jud's done said he's the one he saw. . . ."

Deputy Biderbeck studied the crowd, slowly but steadily turning ugly. It could quickly become a lynch mob, take his prisoner from him — a prisoner that duty demanded he keep alive.

There were other reasons, too, pride for one, but mostly he wanted to see Albert Toon's face when he told the famous lawman he had already captured the killer of his brother. Albert, a U.S. deputy marshal, for all his big reputation could not boast of having brought in a killer so swiftly.

Thing to do was hurry and get his man locked in a cell where he would be comparatively safe. Albert Toon would be riding in soon. The lawman had just left Harmony after a visit with his brother. He couldn't have gotten far.

His face hardened. "We'll have no more of that kind of talk, Bert!" he said, singling out one of the men who had spoken. "This prisoner's goin' to get protection from me same as any of you honest citizens would, was you to get yourself in trouble around here. The judge'll do the decidin' about when there's to be a hangin'." He paused, let his eyes sweep across the crowd. "Now,

24

stand back. Give us room. Don't want nobody hurt."

He moved forward, motioned for Campion and the others to follow. Arms flung wide, he cleared a path. The people fell back, impressed by his businesslike determination.

"That Willis sure is takin' over, ain't he?" someone murmured admiringly.

Matt saw Biderbeck smile contentedly. The deputy was congratulating himself on the wisdom of his decision. Likely he was already pinning Henry Toon's badge on his shirt, was thinking of how he would spend the additional salary.

They crossed the street and entered the hot, cramped quarters of the marshal's office and jail. Biderbeck stepped to one side, allowing Campion, the Mexican deputy, and the two citizens who had helped back in the café, to enter. He then blocked the doorway.

"Sorry folks, but I'll have to keep the rest of you outside. We got important work to do. Only man I want to see now is Jud Wooster."

"Right here, Willie!" a man sang out, and elbowed his way to the fore.

Biderbeck flushed, frowned. Apparently he disliked being called Willie. "Took you long enough to get here," he said, stiffly.

25

"Been standin' right here listenin' to you spout," Wooster said. "Was it election time, I'd say you was runnin' for somethin'.."

Biderbeck eyed him sternly. "This ain't no time for jokin'! You ought to know that bein' a witness to a murder is real important business."

Wooster, a thin, narrow-faced man, grinned, placed his hands on his hips. "Reckon my ol' woman and kids figures it's real important I keep workin' so's they can eat, too," he said in a voice all could hear. "Feller just can't up and leave his diggin's every time somebody hollers jump!"

A ripple of laughter ran through the crowd. The lawman jerked his head at Wooster. "Inside," he said, and whipped away from the door.

Campion had stood silent and patient, listening to the exchange in the street while the Mexican deputy and the two other men searched his person thoroughly for more money.

"You find anything?" Biderbeck asked, moving to his desk.

"Nothin'," one of them replied. "Went over him good, boots and all. Some loose change in his pockets. Four or five dollars."

The deputy nodded. "What I figured. He's stashed the rest somewhere and was goin' back after it when things cooled down a mite." He swung to his prisoner. "You got a name?"

"Most folks do," Matt snapped. "Mine's Campion. Matt Campion."

"Where you from?"

"Lots of places. Came to here from Wichita. Give me time to get word back there and I'll prove you've got the wrong man."

"You'll get your chance when the judge gets here," Biderbeck said. "Jud, now you stand over there across the room and take a good look at this jasper. Don't be in no hurry. Don't want you makin' a mistake. Look close — he the man you seen ridin' hell bent away from the killin's?"

Campion stared at Jud Wooster. He recognized him now — the man at the livery barn where he had stabled the sorrel. He had spoken to him briefly, given him instructions as to the care he desired for the big red horse. Other than that he was a stranger. He watched Wooster cock his head first to one side, then the other.

"Well?" the deputy demanded, his tone impatient. "What about it?"

Wooster, having his moment of glory, hesitated. "Got to be sure," he muttered. "You just told me that. Don't figure to be

27

no part of sendin' the wrong man to a hangin'.' "

"Man ought to know what he seen," Biderbeck grumbled.

The stable-owner ignored the remark. He moved to the door, squinted hard at Campion. He straightened suddenly.

"That's him, sure enough!" he announced in a loud voice. "He's the one I seen. Him on that big sorrel with the white stockin's. Ain't no mistake!"

3

Matt Campion sat on the edge of his cot and listened to the low hubbub of voices in the street. In the full dark he could see nothing beyond the dimly lit area of the marshal's office, but there was a considerable crowd gathered in front. More lynch talk, he guessed.

He arose, irritably began to pace the narrow length of his cell. Damn them — let them go ahead! They might as well! They had him all split, stuffed, and ready for roasting, anyway. Wouldn't make any difference in the long run whether he was dangled from a rope with or without the legal blessing of a circuit judge. He'd be just as dead.

He had been a fool to let them take him. He should have taken his chances, put up a fight — if not in that café where the opportunity hadn't been exactly right, then in the street when they were crossing over or else when they had first entered the jail. But he hadn't been thinking straight. He had wanted things started right in this new country and he had been sure the witness they had raked up would admit he had made a mistake. It hadn't worked out that way. That fool stableman — Jud Wooster — had lied, had insisted he was the man he had seen riding away from the murder.

Either Wooster was blind or he was hiding something. Maybe he was a party to the killings himself and was covering up, protecting himself and the man or men who were in it with him. And the marshal and the whole town believed him. Matt Campion swore savagely. He was in one hell of a predicament; like a man caught at the end of a box canyon with a wounded grizzly closing in.

He had no illusions as to his chances when it came to a trial before a judge. It would mean nothing. A town marshal dead, not to mention the bank clerk; a reputable businessman who was positive in his claim to have seen the man who committed the murders. Add to that an ambitious deputy bucking for the dead marshal's job by showing off his dedication and efficiency in handling the matter, and a man realized what a stacked deck actually was!

Which still wasn't all of it; the dead

marshal's brother, Albert Toon, was a government marshal. The Mantracker, they called him. He had a big reputation for never losing his man, once he set out after him. Like a bulldog, everyone said — he was the sort that never quit. Campion had heard of him. He was en route to Harmony that very moment and should arrive sometime during the night. He had been sent for when the murder was discovered. But his services wouldn't be needed now; Willis Biderbeck had a prisoner all set to present to him.

The blocky shape of the deputy suddenly filled the doorway. Beyond him in the street voices were dying away. The crowd was breaking up. The lawman had convinced them to let the judge do the job; they'd get their hanging party. Biderbeck stood in the opening for a long minute, his eyes following the departing citizens. Then he turned, and moving to his desk sat down. He removed his hat, ran a palm over his balding head.

"Close there for a bit," he murmured. "Figured maybe we had us some trouble."

Campion shrugged. "Don't see as it makes much difference."

The deputy looked up. "You'll get a trial. And it'll be a fair one."

31

Campion snorted. "Who you joshing, Deputy? I'm standing on that gallows right now."

"You'll have your chance to prove whether you're innocent or guilty," Biderbeck insisted doggedly.

"Prove — how? Take a couple of weeks to get word back and forth to Wichita. Nobody else around here knows me. You think that judge will give me time to do that — to dig up my proof? Will you and the rest of the people in this town wait?"

Biderbeck squirmed uncomfortably. "This is a law-abidin' community, and we —"

"Don't give me that!" Campion snarled. "I'm getting railroaded and you know it! Don't know where this Wooster fits in but he sure as hell never saw me — and I've got a hunch you know that only you're not saying anything because you've got ideas; you've got your own little coffee mill to grind and it suits you best to let things stand as they are."

Biderbeck blinked his owlish eyes. "Reckon I'll have to admit there's a mighty strong case against you. But I ain't sayin' nothin' one way or another. Ain't my job. I'm just doin' what's expected of the law —"

"Law's expected to be honest!" Campion

shot back. "If you want to keep it that way, then start doing some digging. Send somebody to the nearest telegraph office and get in touch with people I know in Wichita. I'll give you the names."

"Take days, maybe weeks," Biderbeck said absently. "Judge'll only be here for tomorrow. And the marshal's brother is ridin' in right now."

Campion brushed away the sweat that had built up on his forehead. "What's he got to do with it? You interested in seeing things done right or in making yourself look like a big man to him?"

Biderbeck's face colored. "You got no call to say somethin' like that."

Campion's laugh was harsh. "I don't? Hell, I'm just the sacrifice goat in this deal. You're flat out afraid to try and get the proof I'm asking for."

"Maybe you got proof and maybe you ain't," the deputy said. "Could be you're just stallin', just sayin' all this, hopin' somethin' will turn up."

"Use your head, Deputy! If I had killed and robbed those two men, you think I'd come within a hundred miles of this town? You know I wouldn't — I'd cut and run the other way, fast as I could travel."

"Unless you wanted to play it real cozy, or

maybe didn't know the country around here. Not many towns in this part of the Territory. Man needin' grub and water would have to come to Harmony. Next place is two hundred miles north.

"Anyway, this is all a lot of palaverin' over nothin'. We've got a witness and there ain't no reason to doubt him. I'd say the chances we've got the right man are mighty good."

"And if I'm not?"

Biderbeck shifted his round shoulders. "Ain't very often an innocent man gets hung. Usually the law's right."

"But sometimes it makes a mistake."

Biderbeck said, "Sure, I reckon it does. Tough when that happens. Tough for everybody."

"But mostly for the man dangling at the end of the rope," Campion said grimly, and turned away.

He resumed his seat on the edge of the slatted cot. There was no use trying to reason with Biderbeck, or trusting to the honesty of the soon-to-arrive circuit judge. The old way of things, where a man looked out for himself, was the best — and the only answer. Thing to do was figure a means of escape. It wouldn't be easy. The deputy was cagey and he wasn't going to miss his hour of glory if he could help it.

Campion paused in his thoughts: that might be the key — Willis Biderbeck's overwhelming desire for success and recognition!

He glanced at the deputy. Biderbeck apparently planned to spend the night at his desk, taking no chances on his prisoner. That would look good to the townspeople: their marshal personally riding herd all night on the killer, making certain nothing went wrong.

Campion sighed audibly, as a man resigning himself to the inevitable. He swung about, stretched full length on the cot. He eyed the deputy covertly. Best not to rush matters — and he needed time to think his plan through completely.

4

An hour later Matt Campion stirred, sat up. He got lazily to his feet, walked to the front of his cell. He was ready. Willis Biderbeck dozed in his swivel chair, hat pulled down over his eyes to shut out the light from a lamp burning on the desk. The street and the town beyond the open doorway were quiet.

"Marshal," Matt called.

The deputy came awake instantly. His boot heels hit the floor with a solid thud and he glanced about hurriedly.

"It's me, Marshal," Campion said. "Hate to bother you but I'd sure be obliged for a drink of water."

Biderbeck groaned, rose, moved to the bucket and tin dipper in the corner behind the desk. He served himself and then carried the container, brimful, to his prisoner.

Campion accepted it, drank it down quickly. "Appreciate that, Marshal," he said, backing to the cot and sitting down. "You're not like a lot of lawmen I've run into. Most of them like to slap a man around some, make things tough for them. Sure can't say that about you."

Biderbeck nodded. "No sense to it, that I can see. You had plenty of run-ins with the law before this?"

"My share," Matt drawled, then added, "Kind of looks like this will be my last one."

Biderbeck, again at his desk, looked up. "That mean you're admittin' to the kill-in's?"

Campion shrugged. "Keep remembering what you said about having a witness. Reckon that adds up to not much chance for me to beat this one."

"Tough band to beat in any game," the deputy said, his voice pleased. After a moment he said, "Anything I can do for you?"

Campion laughed bitterly. "Sort of a last request, that it, Marshal?"

"Was only tryin' to be decent," Biderbeck replied, injured. "Man sometimes has a few things he wants done before it's too late."

"Reckon that's right. How much time will I have, figuring that judge sentences me to a hanging?"

"Maybe 'til next mornin'. Or he could want it done quick on account of the way people are feelin'. We already got us a gallows," he added as an afterthought. "Was built two years ago."

Matt let the subject ride for a minute. Then, "You got me thinking, Marshal. There are a couple of things I ought to do. Need to write some letters — two, I reckon. Could you let me have some writing tools?"

Biderbeck said, "Sure thing. Got some paper and envelopes right here in the desk."

He jerked open one of the drawers, clawed around a bit and came up with the requested items. Campion watched him move up to the bars, thrust them through one of the openings. The deputy was careful to stay well back.

Campion reached for the papers. "Obliged to you. Like I said, you're a good man, one that makes a fellow respect the law. Glad I'm going to be a part of getting you the marshal job."

"Ain't no reason why I won't get it now," Biderbeck said. "Leastwise, none that I can see —"

"Say!" Matt exclaimed suddenly. "Just maybe I can help you a little more, sort of tie this thing up tight for you."

He watched the lawman's reaction from the corner of his eye. Biderbeck straightened slowly, his interest aroused. "Meanin' what?"

"How'd it be if I was to give you a written confession, one saying I did those killings and took that money? Expect that would go a long way toward making you the top lawman around here, wouldn't it?"

Willis Biderbeck glowed. "Would, for a fact! Was I to go before that judge in the mornin' with everythin' all cut and dried . . ." His words trailed off as he contemplated the effect it would have upon everyone concerned.

"You'd be getting all the credit for it, for the whole works, capturing me, the confession, everything. You wouldn't need to depend on a witness or anything else."

The deputy's smile dimmed slightly. "Why would you be doin' this?"

Campion moved his shoulders. "Why not? Can't see as it would make any difference to me. And I'm a man who likes to return favors. Never did set comfortable when I owed a man a debt."

Biderbeck appeared uninterested in the answer to the question he had voiced. "Sure would be a feather in my cap," he murmured.

"Just you hand me another piece of paper," Matt said, and then played his trump card. "Couple more things I'll put in that confession; little deals over in Kansas and Texas I got mixed up in. You might as well get credit for cleaning them up, too. Be some reward money due you there."

Biderbeck hastened to provide the necessary sheet of paper. Matt watched him cross the room to the cell. He was not quite so cautious this time, allowing Campion to reach through the bars. Matt played it straight, made no suspicious moves. The moment was not yet ripe. He must wait until there could be no slip-up, for he would get no second chance. But Willis Biderbeck had taken the bait; the mention of reward money had been the clincher.

"Any special way I ought to start this? Never had any experience writing a confession."

Biderbeck folded his arms across his chest and studied the rain-defaced ceiling. "No special way that I know of. Just say what you done and how you done it. Better mention the name of them towns in Texas and Kansas where the other killin's took place. And the names of the men that got killed." He paused, thought for a moment. "Reckon that's all we'll need. Oh, one thing, don't forget to write down that you done this without no proddin' from me. Judges don't like it much when a lawman makes a pris'ner confess."

"Sure. I'll put it in here that it was my own idea."

Willis Biderbeck nodded. He wet his lips, smiled contentedly. He was a man already busy counting his unhatched ducklings, certain of their existence. Campion, using the slatted cot as a table, began to write. He had no idea of how much time he could plan on. It could be the balance of the night, or it could be only minutes. He preferred to consider it on the latter basis.

He completed his task, got to his feet. The deputy had moved to the doorway, was looking out into the night, visualizing, no doubt, the many fine things that now would come to him.

"Marshal," Matt called. "Got it all down. Like for you to look it over, see if it's the way you want. Then I think you're supposed to sign as a witness."

Biderbeck wheeled hurriedly, crossed the room in eager strides. He halted next to the bars, extended his hand for the sheet of paper. Campion felt his nerves tighten briefly, then relax as the old coolness swept through him. This was the critical moment; what happened next determined whether he would live or die.

"Hope you can read it," he said, his voice low. "Not much with a pencil and paper in the first place. And leaning over, using that cot for a table . . ."

"I can read it," Biderbeck said confidently. "Don't you worry none about that. Main thing —"

Matt Campion's arm shot out with the suddenness of a striking rattlesnake. His powerful fingers closed upon the deputy's collar. He jerked hard, throwing all his strength into the motion. Biderbeck slammed up against the unyielding iron bars of the cell. Breath gushed from his mouth in an explosive gasp and his head snapped forward.

Campion snatched at the weapon on the lawman's hip. He felt the cool metal of it in his hand, and a deep feeling of relief sped through him. The bad moment was past — that dangerous fragment of time when he reached for Biderbeck. Had he misjudged, had his fingers slipped, lost their purchase, all would have gone for nothing. The lawman would not a second time fall for any trick.

He held tight to the man, waited for him to collect his scattered wits. Biderbeck's head had not struck the bars too hard; he was only stunned. After a long minute he stirred, regained himself. He grew rigid as he realized what had happened — and recognized the hard, round pressure against his back for what it was.

Campion, his voice a harsh threat, said, "You've got a choice, Deputy. Either you'll be alive two minutes from now, or you'll be dead."

Biderbeck trembled in Campion's grasp, from anger or from fear — there was no knowing which.

"Get the keys off your desk. Open this cell."

Biderbeck found a smattering of courage. "What if I won't? You'd be crazy if you shot me. . . ."

"That's the choice I told you about. I will shoot. I'll kill you, Deputy, sure as you're standing there. And why not? They can only hang me once."

Biderbeck's shoulders went down in defeat. The logic of the argument was not lost on him. He bobbed his head wearily. "All right, but you won't be gettin' far. I promise you that."

"Be my worry," Campion said. "Now get those keys. You make a run for that door and I'll drop you before you take three steps."

The lawman crossed the room slowly. He

picked up the keys, wheeled, and returned. His face was bright red, Matt noticed, and likely he was already building his story of how he had been tricked. Things were going to be tough for Willis Biderbeck's pride.

The cell door swung open. Campion stepped out quickly. He motioned the deputy inside, closed the grating and locked it. He tossed the keys into the water bucket.

The sound of an approaching horse brought Matt Campion around. He reached the front window in two long strides, looked out into the street. The view was restricted and he could see nothing. He glanced over his shoulder at Biderbeck.

"One peep out of you and I'll bend this gun barrel over your head!" he warned.

He moved to the door of the jail, closed it softly. Then, gliding to the dark corner adjacent, he drew himself close to the wall. The horse had halted; whether it was somewhere down the street or at the hitch rack fronting the building, he could not tell. He waited, riding out the slow, dragging moments. Escape had been so near . . . so close . . . and now this. He slid a glance at Biderbeck. The deputy had settled down on the cot, his eyes glued to the door.

Campion heard the scuff of boots on the outside landing. He flattened himself against

44

the wall, pulling deeper into the corner. The latch lifted, the panel swung back. Campion saw the dark, bulky shape of a man step into the dimly lit room. At that instant Willis Biderbeck yelled.

"Mr. Toon — look out!"

Campion brought his gun down in a short, swift arc. It thudded against the man's head, knocked his hat skittering off into a corner, dropped him heavily to the floor.

"That's Mr. Toon!" Biderbeck said in a shocked voice. "You've — you've killed him!"

The Mantracker — the big lawman they had talked about. Campion smiled grimly. He kicked the door closed with his heel, knelt beside the man. He placed his head against Toon's breast. The lawman wasn't dead, only unconscious. Again that tight smile crossed Campion's lips. He plucked Toon's pistol from its holster, threw it to one side. Then, taking the man by the shoulders, he dragged him into the unoccupied cell next to Biderbeck and locked the door.

He returned to the desk, moving hurriedly now. He could not afford to press his luck any harder. The next interruption might not pan out so well for him. He jerked out the drawers until he found his own pistol and exchanged it for the one he had in his hand. He swung toward the door, paused.

"You've got a thousand dollars of mine," he said to Biderbeck. "Don't forget it. I'll be back and collect it later."

"You won't get far!" the deputy shrilled from the shadows of his cell. "He'll be after you now! Not only be me and a posse, but Mr. Toon himself!"

"Time you get somebody awake and down here, I'll be a long way off," Campion said.

"Makes no difference," Biderbeck said. "He'll hunt you down. He'll find you."

"When he does," Campion said drily, "I'll have the real killer with me. Tell him that."

5

Campion stepped out into the street. He remained close to the building, first having his look up and down the deserted, dusty lane. There was little of the new moon, and Harmony, except for its two larger saloons, lay quiet and dark. The Mantracker's horse, a huge, black-and-white paint, stood at the rack next to the jail. Other than him and the half-dozen or so that stood, hipshot, in front of the saloons, the street was empty.

He pulled the door closed behind him, knowing he could expect Willis Biderbeck to begin yelling immediately. That worried him little. The jail was constructed of adobe with walls two feet thick, and since it stood at the extreme west end of the settlement, there was no likelihood of his being heard at that hour.

He turned then and started at a trot for the stable where he had left the sorrel. There he also should find Jud Wooster, the man who claimed to have seen him near the killings. Before he rode out he meant to have a talk with the stable-owner; he represented the one possibility of getting a line on the real murderer.

He reached the livery barn without encountering anyone and let himself in through the side door. He first sought out the sorrel and quietly saddled and bridled the big red horse, making him ready for travel. Although the sorrel had garnered little rest in the short time he had been in a stall, he had been fed and watered and had benefited from the rubdown Campion had ordered for him. Leaving the horse ready, Campion then walked silently to the office and occasional living quarters where he hoped to find Wooster.

He was in luck. He had considered the possibility of the stableman being absent, that he might have chosen that night to stay home, or perhaps to visit one of the saloons. But he was there. When Matt pushed open the crudely made door to the office, Wooster, clothed only in drawers, lay sleeping on a cot. Checking hastily to be certain there was no one else about, Matt leaned down, shook the man awake. Wooster sat up with a start.

"Who is it? What's wrong?"

Campion moved to the end of the bed where the dim light from a lantern hanging outside in the stable runway could fall across his face.

"It's me — Campion. We've got some talking to do."

"Campion!" Wooster echoed, his eyes spreading into round circles of alarm. "I thought —"

"You thought I was locked up in jail. I'm not. I'm right here — and don't get any fancy ideas. I'm holding a gun on you."

Wooster stiffened as his fear rose. "You got no cause to jump me! I only told what I seen —"

"You didn't see me!" Campion snapped impatiently. "Get that straight. And that's what I'm here for. Why did you lie about it?"

"I didn't lie —"

Campion's open palm cracked smartly against the stableman's cheek. "You never saw me," he said in a low, grinding voice. "If you claim you did, then you're sure as hell lying! I wasn't anywhere near that killing. Now, who're you covering up for? You mixed up in it?"

"God as my witness, no! And I ain't coverin' nobody neither. I seen you, Campion — or sure thought I did. Was a big man on a sorrel. One with white stockin's. I'd swear it was you!"

"But you weren't close enough to see for sure?"

"Not exactly close enough to see the man's face, if that's what you're drivin' at. But it sure looked like you on that horse. . . ."

"That kind of witness talk is about to get me hung," Campion said angrily. "Lot of men my size in this country. And plenty of sorrels with white stockings."

"But I seen —"

"That's what I want to know; exactly what did you see? What kind of outfit was this man wearing?"

"Well, can't say that exactly either. Too far off, but he was big —"

Campion swore in disgust. "About all you know is that you saw a man on a sorrel horse — and not much more. You dead sure he was the man who did the killing?"

"Sure am sure of that! He was comin' from where it happened. And movin' fast. Couldn't've been nobody else."

"He see you?"

"Nope, don't think so."

"And he rode north?"

"Yep, followin' the old stage road," Wooster said, nodding vigorously.

50

"That don't make sense," Campion said, his voice doubtful. "Seems to me a man wanting to get away fast would make a run for the Mexican border."

Wooster shrugged. "Maybe, but could be he wasn't set for that kind of a trip. Tough country, that way. Man can't hardly carry enough grub and water to get him to the next town. Besides, everybody'd guess he'd he headin' that way."

It made sense then to Campion. He thought for a moment. "About all you can tell me is that a man my size, forking a sorrel like mine, rode north. Nothing else."

"Reckon that's all I can say about it."

Campion straightened up. "Pretty slim evidence to hang a man on — and that's about what you did to me. Now listen, Wooster. Your mouth has fixed me so's I've got a murder charge hanging over my head. Only thing I can do is try to run the real killer down. No other way I can clear myself."

"Was only doin' what I thought was right. . . ."

"Maybe. I've still got some doubts. Anyway, come morning, you go see Biderbeck and tell him you're not sure it was me you saw. Make it plain, understand? Tell him what you told me — and then you start

51

praying I catch up to this man on a sorrel. . . ."

Wooster said, "Yes, sir. What — what did you do to Willis?"

"Locked him in one of his cells. He's not hurt. But don't go looking for him tonight. I want him to stay put until morning. And don't think you can sneak out on me, either, Wooster! I figure on doing some prowling around town before I ride out. I'll be watching this place."

"I'll wait," Wooster said. "I sure will."

Campion moved toward the door. "You'll find that big lawman, Mantracker they call him, in the cell next to Biderbeck. Make sure he hears what you tell the deputy."

The stableman was momentarily speechless. Then, "You got Albert Toon locked up down there, too?"

"That's what I said."

"Great God!" Wooster breathed. "You sure do bite off big chunks —"

"Mind what I told you," Campion warned, opening the door. "Stay right here until daylight, then go tell both of them what you told me."

"Yes, sir," Wooster agreed quickly.

Campion stepped out into the runway. He hastened to the sorrel. Taking up the reins, he led the horse to the wide, double entrance and, opening the right hand side, looked carefully about. The town still lay silent. One of the saloons was now dark, its patrons apparently having drifted on to the other. At the far end of town he could see the indistinct shape of the Mantracker's barrel-bodied paint horse. It had not moved from the hitch rack fronting the jail.

Campion entered the street, swung onto the saddle. Wheeling about, he struck north at a fast walk, resisting the urge to break the sorrel into a gallop until he was well away from the settlement. He raised his eyes, looked into the shadowy distance. Somewhere ahead was a man on a red horse — a killer for whose deeds he was being blamed.

Albert Toon was squat, ruddy-faced and blue-eyed. He was dressed in a faded blue suit, derby hat, a soiled gray shirt with a tie-less celluloid collar. His stubby fingers toyed restlessly with a heavy gold watch chain that looped across his belly as he listened to Willis Biderbeck, the deputy.

"That's the way it happened, Mr. Toon. Your brother was ridin' guard with the bank messenger to the mine. The robber held them up and took the payroll money. He shot them both in the head, usin' a scattergun, then he piled them into the buggy and set it afire. Wasn't much left but we give them a reg'lar funeral anyway."

Toon allowed his expressionless, flat gaze to sweep the men who had crowded into the jail, settling it upon the one they called Jud. He was the one who had found them locked in the cells and released them.

"This Campion," he said in a slow, heavily accented voice, "you iss sure he rode north, eh?"

"Yes, sir, Mr. Toon," Wooster replied quickly. "I figure it's the only way he could've gone."

The lawman blinked. "You did not see him?"

"No, sir. Didn't actually watch him ride off, but from what he was thinkin' . . ."

Toon shrugged his ponderous shoulders. Few things upset his plodding, tranquil mind. Stupidity was one of them — and these were stupid men: the deputy, the stable-keeper, the whole bunch. He shifted his glance to Biderbeck.

"But you are sure he iss the guilty man?"

"No doubt of it," the lawman said. "Jud here is a witness. Seen him ridin' away from where it happened. Ain't that right, Jud?"

Wooster frowned, hesitated. Toon came back to him with his piercing, pressing stare.

"Well?"

54

"Yes, sir," the stableman said hurriedly. "Big man on a sorrel horse. I sure seen him."

Toon grunted. That settled it. Campion was his man — and he must be brought in. Not just because Hendrick had been his brother; actually Hendrick had always resented him and there had been little affection between them. But a crime had been committed and it was his job to bring in the transgressor.

"Won't take no more'n a few minutes to get a posse together, Marshal," Biderbeck said, all business. "Can get us a dozen men, at least."

Toon wagged his round head. "It iss not needed. This I will do my own self."

"But with a posse —"

"The man has three, four hour start," Toon explained patiently. "A posse will be no good now. It iss better I go alone. A posse he will watch for — one man he will not notice."

"Be glad to go along with you myself," Biderbeck said, trying a different tack. "Two of us might be better'n one."

"No," Toon said wearily. "It iss for me by myself."

Abruptly, he was finished with talk. He spun on his heel, moved out into the street.

Without looking at the men who crowded through the doorway after him, he wheeled to his horse. He jerked the reins free of the rack, swung onto the saddle, and pointed the paint north. His head ached slightly from the blow Matt Campion had dealt him, but he ignored it. His time would come.

6

It was going to be hot.

Matt Campion pulled the sorrel to a halt beside an almost bare mesquite and glanced toward the east. The sun was just breaking over the rim of the desert and beginning its swing across the cloudless, steel-blue sky. Another hour or two and he would be wilting under its merciless blast.

He was glad it was finally light. Now he could look for and perhaps find the hoofprints of the fleeing killer's horse. Wooster had said the man had taken an old, unused stagecoach road. In the darkness he had failed to locate it. Now he should have better luck.

He let his eyes scan the rocky, almost barren land. From where he had halted he could look out upon the flow of a narrow valley. To his back the choppy hills ran on for a time and then gradually lifted into a blue haze of higher, peaked mountains. The road, he reasoned, would likely follow up the floor of the valley, pursuing the line of least resistance.

He swung the gelding away from the mesquite and struck out at right angles for the bottom of the swale. He was now heading due east and would necessarily lose time; but it could not be helped. He must know definitely that the man he hunted was still ahead, and that could only be proved by the tracks of his horse in the loose dust and sand.

He rode on steadily, his wide-brimmed hat pulled down over his eyes to shut out the direct sun. He did not push the sorrel hard, mindful of the fact the red horse had gotten only a small amount of rest and was still in no condition for a long, hard trip. But rest would come later, for both of them; just as soon as he was certain they were on the right trail.

Near an hour later he crossed the twin, almost obliterated ruts of the abandoned roadway. He pulled up, dropped from the saddle. Going to his haunches, he began to search about in the shallow dust. In a flat stretch almost a hundred yards farther along than where he had first broached the road, he found what he was looking for: the fresh prints of a running horse.

He had no way of telling exactly how old they were, but they were less than a day. The edges were still sharp and the small depressions caused by the frog in the horse's hoofs were yet distinct and not softened by the winds.

Campion rose to his feet, threw his glance ahead across the flat, empty land. That there was a rider in front of him was now apparent. That he had passed that way within the last twenty-four hours was also most likely; that he was the man he sought was only guesswork.

He had no reason to believe Jud Wooster had lied to him. The stableman had been frightened and the truth would have been a normal thing to expect. But there could be other riders heading north. The west was filled with drifters, saddlebums, coming from everywhere, going to nowhere in particular. And, too, the prints could have been made by some cowpuncher going back to his home ranch after a few days in town.

He considered it all, concluded he had no choice but to assume it was the killer. Logical thing to do was push on, endeavor to catch up at least near enough for a glimpse of the horse. If the animal proved to be a sorrel, then he could reasonably expect the rider to be the one he wanted. If it were not

— he shrugged and turned to his mount —
if not, it meant starting all over. But he
would not think of that now. He would
jump that arroyo when he came to it.

He put the sorrel to a slow, easy lope, a
pace that he knew the horse favored and
that would not tire him to any extent. He
kept to the smoother, easier-traveled surface
of the old road. Heat was beginning to make
itself felt more now and soon he would have
to be pulling in to make allowances for the
red. The few hours in the stable had helped
him considerably but had not been long
enough to really count.

A fact grew suddenly in Campion's mind:
since Jud Wooster had not said *when* he saw
a man on a sorrel riding north, Matt had
no idea of how great a start the rider had
on him. It could be a half a day, a full day
— or even more. Somehow the question had
slipped his mind while he was talking with
the stableman. And if the killer hadn't
paused to rest his horse, he could be well
beyond reach by that hour.

Campion swore. It was all pretty thin, and
there were far too many *if*s sprinkled
through his assumptions and scheme; still,
it was a gamble he must take. One thing he
did recall was Biderbeck saying only one
town of size lay to the north, that there was

nowhere else a man could go. Assuming that was the case, the killer must point directly for that settlement. And persons living there, unused to many strangers, would remember seeing a man on a big red horse. There was that much he could count on.

He wondered how things were going back in Harmony. By this time someone would have discovered Toon and Willis Biderbeck locked in the jail, and released them. It could have happened earlier but he doubted that. The town, as a whole, had been soundly sleeping when he rode out, not counting the drinkers at the saloon, of course. But being drinkers they would have stayed put.

The one possibility was Jud Wooster; he might have screwed up enough courage to leave his bed and go to the lawmen but that, too, was a matter of doubt. Wooster struck Campion as being a careful man and therefore one not given to bravery.

He smiled grimly, thinking of Albert Toon. And he could, in his imagination, think of what the lawman must have said to Deputy Willis Biderbeck when finally they were freed of the cells. He could sympathize with Toon, as he could with any man who had to put up with the Biderbecks and the Woosters of the world.

He no longer felt too bitter toward Harmony and the men who lived in it. They had simply jumped to a conclusion, aided considerably by circumstance and that fool Wooster. It was no uncommon failing in the West. In fact, it occurred pretty much everywhere, he guessed, and to the people of the settlement he did appear to be the guilty man.

And he would continue to, he realized, until he caught and returned the real murderer to them. His overcoming Biderbeck and Toon and his subsequent flight had not helped his position any; but it had been the only course he could follow. If Jud Wooster would tell them all he had instructed him to say, the heat would be off his back, but that, too, was problematical. Being the sort Matt had him figured, the stableman was not likely to admit he was wrong, not when his role as a witness made him the town's most important figure.

None of that would matter if the real killer were brought to justice. And he must be. Campion had no desire to spend the rest of his days with the threat of a hanging on his shoulders. Besides, he had big plans; he still intended to buy that ranch in the Cloverdale area and become a part of the Territory. To do so he must be able to come and go at will, in peace. Only the bringing in of the killer of Henry Toon and the bank clerk would make that possible now. Therefore he could not rest until the chore was completed — and he could allow nothing to interfere.

Near noon the road began to bend toward the low hills and bluffs. A few trees became visible and, to escape the blazing sun and heat for a short rest, Campion headed the steadily tiring sorrel for the nearest one. He was saving the horse as much as he could, aware that the time might come soon when he would need to call upon the big red for a fast, hard sprint. He was not in too good a condition himself, having had little rest in the past twenty-four hours. And thirst was beginning to plague him. There had been no time to fill his canteen — but that wasn't worrying him too much yet; it was the gelding that occupied his attention.

He dismounted in the meager shade of a juniper and loosened the saddle girth so the horse could find more ease. That done, he sprawled out, wondering again about Toon and Biderbeck. A posse would likely be on his trail by that time. It did not disturb him to any extent. He had a good lead, trimmed some to be sure by his riding eastward in search of the stagecoach road. Posses were generally of small consequence, anyway.

63

One or two men were always more effective.

He sat up suddenly. A thin wisp of blue smoke trailing skyward caught his attention. It came from somewhere beyond a stand of bluffs farther west. He studied it for some time, speculating as to its source. He had been told there were no settlements in the area, yet here was evidence of human life. The possible meaning of the fire came to him quickly; it could be the man on the sorrel.

He arose quickly. He tightened the gelding's gear, mounted up and struck off across the choppy hills for the irregular facing of buttes. He was again losing time, cutting his lead on any pursuers, but he felt the sacrifice was worth it. It could mean a sudden finish to the search. An hour later he broke out of the rough country and came upon a wide, flat mesa, and the origin of the smoke.

It was no campfire, no lone rider cooking his meal. Instead he found a small Mexican settlement: a cluster of three adobe huts, a crude corral of juniper and cedar poles, a half a dozen goats that ran loose in the littered yard.

Disappointed, Campion rode in closer. At his appearance a man moved into the doorway of the largest shack, watching him with bright, suspicious eyes. Matt drew to a halt. It could be a lucky break after all; he could fill his canteen, possibly buy a bit of food. He glanced about for a well or spring.

"Water?" he asked, pointing to his empty container.

The Mexican moved his head. He waved toward the distant mountains. "You mus' go there."

Campion shook the canteen to show it was dry. "You got some here? I'll pay you. Like to buy some grub too, if you can spare it."

The Mexican's dark face did not change. "The water barrel is empty, *senor.* Tonight I go to the spring for more. The other *Americano* take all."

Other American!

Campion pushed forward. "This other man — who was he?"

The Mexican shrugged. "I do not know. A rider like yourself."

"What kind of a horse was he on?"

The man pointed at the sorrel. "Very like the one you have, *senor.* A twin, I think."

Campion felt his hopes surge. "How long ago was he here?"

"This morning, almost with the sunrise. But already it was hot. That is why I wait for the night before I go for water."

Campion considered. He was in luck. At

least he knew he was on the right track — the killer was definitely in front of him. No more than six, perhaps seven hours. And since he was not aware of someone trailing him, he likely would halt for the night.

"That man — he keep going north?"

"*Si,* for the north."

"*Gracias,*" Campion said, exercising one of the few words of Spanish he knew, and rode from the yard. He would forget food and the need for water; it was more important to keep on the killer's trail now that he was certain of the man's existence.

He urged the sorrel to a trot, climbed a gentle slope a short distance from the huts, and topped onto a broad, circular knob. He halted there, threw his glance to the north. The land lay broad and empty before him with no living thing stirring beneath the harsh sun. But the killer was out there — somewhere.

Campion twisted about on the saddle, surveyed the country behind him. He stiffened. A lone rider, far to the south, also had paused on the crest of a hill. The sunlight brought him and the mount he bestrode out distinctly; a thick-bodied man on a large black-and-white horse. There could be no mistake.

The Mantracker was on his trail.

7

Campion spurred the sorrel off the hilltop angrily. There was a slim chance Toon had not seen him. He allowed the gelding to plunge downgrade until they reached the floor of the arroyo that cut off toward the east, and there pulled him to a stop.

His feelings exploded suddenly. Damn the luck, anyway! With the killer almost within reach Toon had to show up and complicate matters! Now he must keep an eye on his back trail as well as the one ahead.

His anger cooled quickly and he began to reason things more calmly. It was better to assume that Toon had spotted him and guard against any surprises. How the lawman had managed to draw so near in so short a time was hard to figure — and immediately he understood. He had lost time swinging back and forth in search of the old road; then he had ridden west to investigate the smoke. Toon had wasted no such motion or time.

One more thing was apparent. Jud Wooster had not waited until daylight to seek out Biderbeck and the government lawman. He had gone to the jail as soon as he felt it was safe, apparently not too long after Campion had ridden out.

But there was no point in mulling over it. Albert Toon, the hunter, was on his trail and dangerously close. He could afford no more time loss if he were to overtake and capture the killer before the relentless old lawman closed in and laid him by the heels.

He put the sorrel into motion, sent him trotting slowly down the arroyo. At the first break in its ragged wall he swung the horse out and climbed again to the plateau, which rolled out to the north and east in a vast, broiled carpet of grays and browns and dusty greens.

Involuntarily he glanced over his shoulder. Toon was no longer visible. He, too, had moved on, was now somewhere below the rim of buttes. The paint horse the lawman rode was coming on steadily, doggedly, evidently in much better condition than the sorrel. Matt had only glanced at the big animal when he came out of the jail that morning and his impression now, in retrospect, was that the paint would not be fast, would rather be strong and powerful, with a tremendous fund of endurance. A perfect counterpart for Albert Toon, Campion thought: solid, patient, and stubbornly persistent.

He rode on through the afternoon's wilting heat. The sun was a round, burnished glare in a cloudless field of gleaming metal, sucking every drop of moisture from his body and gradually, but surely, wearing down the sorrel. Campion began to cast anxious glances toward the horizon to the west, trying to estimate how long until the fiery ball would be gone, until sundown and the reviving coolness of night closed over the land.

His mind refused to calculate, and the sun seemed to hang motionless, sink no lower. Campion turned impatient with himself, cursed himself for a fool. He should have taken time to provide himself with water, with food. It would have been smart to swing wide, visit the mountain spring the Mexican had mentioned. But he had been in too much of a hurry, he had been too anxious. He should take a lesson from Albert Toon's book — the steady, plodding, never-give-up Mantracker . . .

Near dark the plateau broke off into a maze of low buttes and arroyos, which in

69

turn led into a wild, disorderly panorama of badlands. Such an area would be difficult traveling in daylight for the worn sorrel, and Campion realized he could never make it in the dark. With the certain knowledge that Albert Toon was not likely to stop with the setting sun, he nevertheless selected a place for a camp and drew to a halt a short time later. The gelding could go another day without water, perhaps, but he must have rest.

He removed his gear from the horse and picketed him in the shade. There was little for him to graze on and, of course, no water, but the sorrel seemed not to mind; he was content just to stand and crop at the thin, sparse growth and be out of the sun.

Campion remained in the shadows until the final break in the dazzling sunlight came and then slowly and painfully climbed to the highest point of the butte beneath which he had made his dry camp. By the time he reached that point of vantage, the smoky gray masses far to the west had swallowed the sun, and the land lay in that darkening period of in-between exact day and precise night.

With the sharp crackling of the gradually cooling rocks in his ears, he looked first to the south, to the general area where he might reasonably expect to see Albert Toon. Only the vast emptiness, ruggedly beautiful in its savage loneliness, met his eyes. He maintained his search until darkness began to deepen the hollows with rich purples and blues, and the shadows along the short hills and buttes lengthened out to blend with the flat land. Only then did he realize there was no point in further observation; he would be unable to distinguish the lawman even if he were out in the open.

He turned his attention then, hopefully, to the north, relying now upon the darkness to point up a campfire that would designate the presence of the killer. Again his probing gaze went unrewarded. If the man for whom he hunted had stopped for the night, he was careful to choose a well-hidden site, one that would shield his campfire from prying eyes. But that would hardly be the case, Campion again reassured himself; the killer did not know he was being followed.

He stayed on the rim of the bluff until it was full dark and the glittering stars had cropped out to hang low in their vast arch of velvet blackness. The breeze had freshened and where there had been stifling, crushing heat only hours before, a faint but marked chill began to set in. The desert was a monstrous, all-powerful force that toyed with all those who dared venture into its endless waste. By day it sweated and broiled and hammered at its trespassers with merciless abandon; at night it went to the other extreme, sweeping the flats and hollows, the ridges and arroyos with a knife-edged wind that cut deep into a man.

Once again at the foot of the butte, Campion checked on the sorrel, found him faring as well as could be expected. He took his blanket roll from the saddle and set about finding a place out of the breeze where he could enjoy a time of rest. He discovered a small pocket in the face of the bluff that would serve his needs well.

Inside it, beyond the reach of the slowly rising wind, he judged it safe to build a fire. Mindful of the distance the glare of flames could carry across the desert, he kept the blaze to a minimum and by using only dry sticks piled beneath the brush.

He lay back finally, exhausted from the long ride in the murderous heat but grateful for the small comfort he was able to procure. His thirst diminished somewhat with the advancing coolness, and he slaked it further to some extent by placing a pebble in his mouth and promoting a better flow of saliva.

Gradually the lowering temperature began

to revitalize his strength, rekindle his spirits. Where, only a short time previously his thoughts had been only of getting free of the sun, of finding a place to rest, he now considered the idea of pressing on. A few hours' rest, and the sorrel might be in shape to continue. He would be unable to move fast, but at least he could travel — and every yard counted. He would take it slow through the wild brake; he could not afford to have the big red horse fall, even stumble, for an injury to him would be fatal to both. But even at a tedious pace they would cover a considerable distance by dawn.

And certainly he should not be halting.

Albert Toon was still coming. The lawman would dog his trail with the stolid, patient persistence that had earned for him his reputation as a peerless manhunter. Albert Toon would not be resting. He would be closing in, slowly but surely moving up with the inexorable constancy of daylight following dark, of the sun rising and setting.

Why run?

The question slipped into his mind with subtle ease. It brought him upright, knotted his brow into a frown. Why run — why not wait for Toon, lie in ambush and, with drawn gun, overcome him? He could then force the lawman to hear him out — and

Toon, being a big-time government marshal, would be reasonable.

It was a logical solution. First, however, he must make it possible for the lawman to find him. He got to his feet, moved away from the bluff. A fire — a campfire — should do the trick. Not a large one, for that might arouse Toon's suspicions; one of ordinary size that a man making camp would build.

He gathered up a supply of wood, carried it to a level place in the center of a cluster of rocks. After he had the flames going, he returned to the hollow for his blanket roll and, with the aid of his hat, he fashioned an illusion of a man stretched out at the edge of the fire's glow, sleeping soundly. That done, he dropped back a distance and critically examined his handiwork. It should fool Albert Toon.

Checking his gun to be sure it was ready, he pulled off a short ways to the right of the pseudo-camp and took up a position in the deep shadows at the base of the butte. From there he could watch the trail to the south and see a man approaching in the distance without revealing his own presence.

He had difficulty in keeping awake. Weariness dragged at his body and his eyes were heavy, continually closing despite his efforts to hold them open. The fire began to dwindle, and ate slowly into the additional supply of sticks he had arranged in an overhung fashion to feed the flames and keep them going. He began to doubt that his signal would last long enough for Toon to be attracted by it; if it did not, there was nothing he could do about it. He could take no chances on showing himself. Toon was clever. He would not approach the camp blindly, would first observe from a distance. . . . Campion stretched carefully. . . . He wished he could move about. . . . It would help him stay awake. . . .

He came up with a sudden jerk. He had been sleeping, he realized, as a mixture of anger and alarm raced through him — for how long he had no idea but, from the position of the stars, he judged it must now be well into the morning hours. He glanced toward the fire. It was down to embers, fanned to glowing depth by the steady, cold breeze. He sat perfectly still, considering. Something had awakened him. Something had brought him out of his exhausted slumber. He remained in the brush, frozen; listened carefully into the night. What had jarred him to consciousness?

In that next moment he knew. His ears, straining into the heart of the desert's hush, caught the sharp, metallic click of a horse's iron shoe coming into contact with a stone. Someone was coming down the trail — and from the south. It could only be Albert Toon.

Campion pulled himself to a crouch cautiously. He palmed his gun, felt the comforting curve of the butt in his hand. He had chosen his position carefully. A man coming into the camp would break out into a small clearing that lay directly ahead. It was no more than ten feet away. Capturing the lawman and disarming him when he came into the open would be easy, simple. Too much so, Campion realized suddenly. Toon was cunning, tricky.

The horse was near. Campion could hear the soft, measured *tunk-a-tunk* of the hoofs, the muted squeak of leather. Off somewhere along the buttes a coyote shrilled into the night — the only other sound. The hoof thuds grew louder. A branch swished; disturbed gravel spilled slowly off into a tiny ravine, clattered hollowly. Alert, cautious, Campion rose to a standing position, keeping the screen of brush before him as he prepared to challenge Toon.

The long, bobbing head of the paint horse came into view, flung up sharply as he beheld the camp, the blanket roll and hat.

Campion resisted the impulse to leap out, to call upon the lawman to throw up his hands. A moment later he was thankful he had not yielded to it. The saddle of the paint was empty.

8

Motionless, absolutely quiet and scarcely breathing, Matt Campion waited in the deep brush. Toon was out there somewhere; Toon who had tried to fool him — and almost had. Campion, his long, lean body a tensed spring, listened into the night. The paint had halted in the center of the clearing. He stood now, head swung low, worn and weary, making little sucking noises as he breathed. The coyote cried again and from a point far to the west came a wailing reply.

A branch snapped.

The sound seemed loud as a gunshot to Campion. He instinctively dropped to a crouch. The noise had come from his right. He realized Toon was circling the clearing slowly, keeping well in the brush. Apparently he was not too certain of the blanket roll and hat decoy, was working around for a closer look. When his ruse with the paint had failed he had changed his tactics.

Campion rode out the tension-filled seconds, hearing the lawman move up step by step. And then abruptly the dark, blocky shape of the man was before him, between him and the clearing. Matt rose swiftly, jammed his gun barrel into Toon's back.

"Don't move," he said in a low, calm voice.

Campion reached forward, pulled the lawman's pistol from its holster and tossed it into the brush. He ran his hands over Toon's body, searching for a hidden weapon, found none. Satisfied, he stepped back.

"Straight ahead. Into the open," he ordered.

Toon sighed heavily, walked slowly into the clearing. In the pale light of the stars the famed manhunter looked to be anything but one of the frontier's most feared and dangerous individuals. Dressed in his dark pants and vest, small hat, and tieless celluloid collar, he appeared more the small-town businessman than anything else.

Some of the rigid tension had left Campion. He was now a tall, loose shape in the night. "Waited here to talk to you," he said. "You're trailing the wrong man."

"So . . ." Toon murmured gently. His eyes were small, black diamonds set much too close in a broad, round face that gave him an almost childlike look. But there was no mistaking the grimness, the utter ruthlessness of the man. It was stamped upon his bitter features as definitely as chiseled rock.

"It iss always the same," he said in a weary, regretful tone. "No man iss ever guilty."

"Happens to be the truth. The man who killed your brother and that bank clerk is on ahead. I'm tracking him."

The lawman shrugged, seemingly having little interest in the moment but Matt saw the sharp interest in his eyes, the hurried calculation as he judged his chances. Doubly vengeful at being out-smarted, he would grasp any opportunity that might lead to escape. Campion fell back a step, his pistol leveled unwavering at Toon's belly.

"Don't try it," Matt warned softly. He ducked his head at a large rock a few paces to the left. "Move over there and sit down. You're going to listen to me."

The lawman complied slowly. Campion took up a position before him, well out of reach, his gun still aimed and cocked.

"What I'm telling you, Toon, is gospel truth. I'm not your man."

The lawman considered Matt through

half-closed lids. "Your name iss Campion," he said laboriously. "You are riding a sorrel horse with white legs. . . . Iss it not so?"

"Yes —"

"You were arrested by the town deputy and put in jail but you escaped. Iss that not so also?"

"They got the wrong man."

"There iss a witness who saw you. He looked at you and said you are the one."

Wooster hadn't come through with the truth. That was evident. Matt guessed he should not have expected him to. The stableman was not the sort to admit he was wrong.

"He lied," Campion said, trying to break through the stone wall of Albert Toon's stolid convictions. "I talked to him before I rode out. Said then he wasn't sure it was me, only that he'd seen a man on a sorrel. You can't hang a man on that."

Toon shifted on the rock. "It iss nothing for me to decide. It iss for the judge. My job only iss to bring you in."

"To bring in the guilty man," Campion corrected him. "Not one who is innocent."

"You are the man!" Toon exclaimed, the sullen anger within him ripping to the surface unexpectedly. "This I know!" A moment later, in his usual calm way, he said,

"It iss for the judge to say. I go by the law. If you are not guilty you will go free."

"Like hell!" Campion snapped, abruptly out of patience. "I haven't got a prayer once I'm locked up in that jail. They've got to hang somebody for those killings and I happened to be handy."

He was realizing he had made no progress at all with the lawman. He had thought Toon would be a reasonable man with whom to deal; he was learning what many before him had discovered: Albert Toon possessed a closed, single-track mind that encompassed nothing but the exact workings of the law — the law as he interpreted it.

And time was wasting. With each passing minute the real killer was drawing farther away. Matt decided to make one final, desperate offer.

"Toon, I'll make you a bargain. The two of us mount up and ride after the man I'm telling you about. We catch him, then it puts me in the clear. If we don't, if there isn't another man on a sorrel on ahead, I'll give up. I'll go back to Harmony with you and there'll be no trouble."

Albert Toon did not stir. He observed Campion in silence, his manner unchanging, his mouth a stiff, colorless slash.

"What do you say, Marshal? We got a deal?"

"The wolf iss now the master," Toon said. "But it will change. Sooner or later I take you to jail. Maybe dead, maybe alive. It does not matter to me."

"You've got a mind thicker than your skull!" Campion said disgustedly. "Stand up. I'm through trying to talk sense to you."

Toon got to his feet. Matt backed to where the paint horse stood, removed the coil of light rope from the saddle. He pointed to a small, hollowed-out place beneath a mesquite.

"Over there. And lay down."

Matt cut the rope into two lengths. Never slackening his vigilance, he bound the lawman's hands together across his belly, tied his booted feet with the other. He took care the knot was wedged securely against the heels. That done he again went to the paint. He pulled off the thick saddlebags, examined their contents for a knife or other weapon. Satisfied they contained nothing Toon could use to free himself with, he placed them beside the man. Toon watched him with his cold, flat eyes.

"It iss better you kill me," he said quietly.

"Maybe," Campion said, unhooking the lawman's canteen. "But killing's not my line

— unless somebody forces my hand."

"I will get loose and come for you," Toon promised in that same unhurried voice.

"Sure, but you're going to be right there for a spell while I go after the real killer. I'll bring him back and make a present of him to you. Oughtn't to take more than a day or two. I'll leave your grub and water handy — after I borrow a little of it."

He caught up the sorrel. Removing his own canteen, he poured a quantity of the water into it. The gelding whickered anxiously at the smell. Campion wet his bandana, swabbed the red's lips and nostrils, then squeezed it dry into his mouth.

Hanging the container back on his saddle, he placed Toon's next to the saddlebags. He knelt down, examined the ropes once more. They were secure. He turned then to the gelding and swung onto the big horse.

"Just don't fret," he said to the lawman. "I'll be back and cut you loose."

Campion rode off after that, feeling the hating eyes of Albert Toon drilling into his shoulders.

9

The sun caught him an hour later as he was climbing a long, gentle slope out of the brakes.

He was pushing the sorrel as hard as he dared. He would have to favor him at all times, and twice Campion had dropped from the saddle and walked ahead of his laboring mount, sparing the animal the more difficult sections of the rough trail.

But he kept on, feeling the heat lift steadily and begin to hammer at him once again. The coolness his body had soaked up during the night hours fled quickly under the harsh, penetrating rays of the sun, and soon there was little of the moisture his body had hoarded left within him.

He must not slacken the pace. The killer was somewhere ahead, and though Albert Toon was at his back, he now presented no immediate problem. A reckoning with him would come later. He recalled the lawman's threatening words: *It is better you kill me.* He could accept the promise in that statement literally, he knew. Toon, if he should somehow manage to free himself and resume the trail, would not stop at mere capture this time. He would shoot to kill. In the old lawman's stubborn mind, he was a murderer, a man who had twice escaped and thus was now a dangerous fugitive.

But forget Toon. He would still be there beneath the mesquite, helpless to do anything except wait. It wouldn't be too hard on him. Campion had tied his hands in front of him, rather than behind his back. The lawman would be able to get to his canteen when he was thirsty, delve into the provisions in his saddlebags if he got hungry. He could survive several days without too much discomfort, and Campion planned on returning in much less time than that.

Near midday, with the merciless sun a molten ball in the sky, Campion found himself again on a broad mesa that flowed endlessly off to a hazy blue horizon. It was a simmering world of glittering sand, glistening rock, and gray, baked desert weeds and scrawny cacti. Nothing moved; no birds, no small animals, not even the usual lizards and occasional snakes were to be noted.

He halted in the brilliant glare, and, once

more dismounting, wet the bandana and moistened the suffering sorrel's mouth. He tried to pour a small amount of the water into the horse's throat but the animal became excited, shook his head violently, and most of the precious liquid was lost. Campion cursed the horse unnecessarily and took a swallow of the canteen's now hot contents. There was little remaining.

He had seen no trail, no tracks that indicated the man he pursued was still ahead. He was sure it could not be otherwise and tried not to worry about it. The way north was the only route. The desert ran interminably to the east and west. Only in the north was there any promise of cessation. But he should have seen some signs of the man's passage, and that failure disturbed him vaguely. Time after time he stared anxiously ahead, hopeful of catching a glimpse of the rider. That moment never came.

Late in the afternoon the worry developed into a fear. Could he have somehow by-passed the killer? Could the man on the sorrel have cut off, permitted Campion to overshoot, and then, turning, doubled back to Harmony? If he believed himself to be in the clear, he could have chosen to do just that. But how could he have known?

And not since the brakes had there been any place where he could have managed to hide out, allow Campion to go by. A man could stand and see for miles on the mesa. It seemed to Matt it would have been impossible. Nor could it have occurred back in the rough, wild area of the brakes. The killer had been far beyond that point when night came. No — he was still ahead. He had to be. Campion guessed it was simply that the man had a much greater lead than he had anticipated. He needed to pick up the pace. He moved on, his red-rimmed eyes smarting from the glare, his face gray and drawn from the heat. Beneath him the sorrel walked slowly, painfully, head low, hoofs dragging across the sand and flat weeds. And then suddenly he halted.

Campion, head sunk into his chest, looked up with a start. A hundred yards ahead, in the cup of a small hollow, stood a canvas-topped wagon. The vehicle canted drunkenly to one side. The left rear wheel had collapsed into a pile of dry splinters. Two horses, heads down, were tethered to the tongue. There was no other sign of life.

Matt Campion felt his hopes surge. Here was water . . . food. Perhaps he could borrow one of the horses, leave the sorrel as a guarantee he would return. . . . He studied the vehicle for a long minute, then raised his voice in a croaking summons.

"Hello — the wagon!"

One of the horses roused, turned to look. There was no movement anywhere else.

"Hello, the wagon! Anybody there?"

The stained, patched canvas moved slightly. Campion saw the flaps at the rear part. The head and shoulders of a young woman appeared. She stared at Campion briefly, then withdrew.

Matt touched the sorrel lightly with his heels, started him forward. He rode in nearer, eyeing the wagon curiously. It had come a long way. The girl he had seen surely wasn't alone. There must be others; a husband, or perhaps father and mother, other members of a family. From the looks of the ground around the two bony horses, they had been stranded several days. He drew the gelding to a halt a dozen paces from the vehicle, leaned forward on the saddle. One of the horses shifted wearily and the sorrel's head came up with a jerk as though noticing the team for the first time.

"You — inside the wagon!" Campion began and choked off the words.

The girl had stepped from behind the shabby vehicle. Apparently she had crawled out on the far side. She held a long, single-barreled shotgun in her hands. It was leveled at Campion.

"Climb down from that horse," she said in a clear, steady voice.

Albert Toon watched Campion head off through the rocks and brush, the man's wide shoulders shifting back and forth with the motion of the sorrel's stride.

He sighed heavily. He had let himself in for it this time — all because he had misjudged a man, had underestimated him. But that was the way it happened some times. A man couldn't hope to be right every time; he could make allowances, try to cover all the possibilities, but now and then things would go wrong. . . .

No matter. It would all work out. Campion had made a bad mistake. . . . Campion had not killed him — and that was going to be fatal. Toon paused, considered that one apparent flaw in the character of the man. For a brief fragment of time the thought centered in his mind that Matt Campion could be telling the truth, that perhaps he was not guilty of the crime and therefore was no killer. But that washed quickly away. Campion was playing it smart, or believed himself to be. It was just plain, old window dressing and he was only trying to cover his trail to make the law think him innocent.

It would cost Campion his life, that mistake. The next time he would take no chances on the man. In the eyes of the law he was guilty, so he would pay. Toon shrugged. He usually made it a point to bring his prisoners in alive despite the stories to the contrary that floated around the country. For one thing it was easier. Lifting a body on and off a horse got mighty tiresome . . . And after a few days in the desert heat, a corpse got plenty ripe. But it was different now where Campion was concerned. He was through fooling with him.

Besides, he'd just as soon the word of Campion escaping from him didn't get out . . . And Campion was bound to tell it if he were brought in alive. Everybody believed those stories about no man ever getting away from Albert Toon and it was only good business to keep people thinking they were true.

He guessed he'd better get started at that rope. No sense in letting Campion get too far ahead. Holding up his bound hands, Toon began tearing at the knot with his broad, strong teeth.

10

The girl's hair was a bright copper in the slanting shafts of the sun. She had it gathered about her head and drawn to a flat bun on the top. In the glaring light it was a vivid swirl of color. Her eyes were blue and her skin possessed that natural transparent fairness of her type, but it had been cruelly dealt with by the desert and had turned painfully ruddy. She was, Campion judged, twenty or twenty-one, and beneath the shapeless dress she had a good figure.

He studied her thoughtfully, making no move to comply. For the moment his own urgent needs and problems were forgotten.

"You don't need that scattergun," he said stiffly.

"I'm not afraid of you," she retorted instantly. "I'm just making sure you stop. We need help."

He nodded his head at the canvas-covered vehicle. "The wagon?"

"Yes, and my father. He's inside and very sick. We've been here for days — almost a week. There was another man rode by here early this morning but he was too far off. I couldn't make him stop. I'm not taking any chances on you."

Campion's attention came into sharp focus. "This other man, was he on a sorrel — a red horse like mine?"

She said, "Yes, he was. Why? He a friend of yours?"

A small sigh slipped from Campion's dry lips. "Not exactly. Just happens I'm in a big hurry to catch up to him."

He felt much better. The killer was still ahead and he was on the right trail. Not too far behind, either. The girl had said early morning. That would put him around twelve hours in the lead. A bit of rest, some water and a meal, and he could start. . . .

"You going to get down?" She emphasized the question with a threatening wave of the shotgun.

Campion frowned.

"Appears you're calling the shots," he said, and came off the saddle, his movements slow and stiff.

The sorrel had smelled the hay scattered in front of the wagon team. He pushed forward eagerly, his steps quickening.

"Horse of mine is hungry," Matt said. "Mind if he eats a little of that timothy?"

She shook her head and gold lights danced in her hair. "There's plenty. But the water is all gone."

He saw her eyes touch the canteen hanging from his saddle. Ignoring the shotgun, he caught up with the gelding, already nuzzling into the hay, unhooked the container and handed it to her.

"Not much left but you're welcome to it."

"Thank you," she murmured gravely. "My father —"

She whirled swiftly and, abandoning the old shotgun to the side of the wagon, parted the canvas flaps and climbed inside. Campion heard her say something, almost missed the reply of a low, weak voice. He stepped to the end of the vehicle and looked in.

The trapped air was sweltering, heavy with the odor of sickness and medicine. A thin, gray-faced man, his eyes no more than deep, glittering coals in black-encircled pockets, lay on a pallet. The girl was holding a cup containing some of the water to his mouth. He appeared to be in a bad way.

"Enough," he muttered. "Save some for yourself."

"There's plenty, Papa," she said.

94

A tired smile tugged at his pinched lips. "You never could lie to me, Della. You know that."

He saw Campion at that moment. Again that worn smile crossed his face. "Thank you, sir, whoever you are, for stopping. It has been hard for my girl."

"Now, Papa," she protested. "It's been no harder for me than for you. Anyway, it's all over now. Help has come. Soon everything will be all right." She turned to Matt. "You will help us, won't you, Mister — Mister —"

"Campion. Matt Campion."

"Won't you, Mr. Campion?"

He hesitated, then said, "Do what I can."

"Thank you," the ailing man said. "My name is Joshua Stockton. And my daughter Della, sir. We were —"

"Never mind," the girl broke in gently. "I'll explain everything to Mr. Campion. You try to sleep."

She moved back to the end of the wagon. Campion brushed the flaps aside, lifted her down. She had a small, firm waist beneath the loose folds of her dress, and he marveled that his two hands completely girdled it. He motioned her to one side.

"Why don't you jerk that canvas up, let some air inside the wagon? So hot in there I don't see how he can breathe."

She turned her set, serious face to him. "I know. I wanted to do that but he objected. Said the heat felt good." Her voice caught and she moved away from him abruptly, looking toward the east. "He's so very sick," she said in a despairing voice. "If I don't get him to a doctor soon —"

"Where were you headed?" Campion asked. "How did you happen to get here? Expect this is one of the worst stretches of country in the Territory."

"We were going to Santa Fe, from California. We were told this was the shortest route — but nobody told us what it would be like, that there were no towns, only miles and miles of desert with no water anywhere." She came back to face him. "Do you know the country well? Can we get water somewhere close? The horses need it badly, too. Is there a town we can reach?"

Campion did not immediately reply to her torrent of anxious questions, and she guessed what his answer would be from that reluctance. He watched the newborn hope die in her eyes, saw her shoulders go down in defeat.

"Stranger here myself," he said. "Fact is, I'm not much better off than you folks."

"Then why are you —"

"Mentioned it before. I'm following a man — one I've got to catch up to."

"The one you asked about — the one on the sorrel?"

Campion nodded. "He's twelve hours ahead of me. Means I've got to keep going or I'll lose him." He let it go at that, made no further explanation.

"I see," Della said tonelessly.

"Wish there was something I could do to help. You don't have a spare wheel?"

"No — nothing."

He looked at her closely, his heart aching for her. She was so small, seemed so helpless and now so utterly alone. She was fighting a losing battle where her father was concerned. The smell of death lay heavy inside the wagon; whatever it was that ailed Joshua Stockton would soon claim him. Of that she was unaware, Campion realized.

It was a sad thing — still, what could he do about it, even if he were not pressed for time? He had his own problems, a need to push on, keep after the killer until he overtook and captured him. His own life depended upon it.

But could he, with clear conscience, just ride off and leave Della Stockton to face her troubles alone? If there were a chance, even a slim one, that somebody else might ride by, someone who could lend a hand, he might feel better about it. But they were in a land where no man ventured without cause or reason. It was far off the usual trail and weeks could pass before another rider passed that way.

Nor could he rely too much on returning himself in the next few days. His plans called for it, since he had Albert Toon to consider — but things could go wrong; a man who had killed twice in cold blood would not surrender meekly.

He stirred impatiently, suddenly irritated that such a problem should be forced upon him. Any other time he would have been glad to help; but now, with the man he must, without fail, overtake, just hours ahead. . . . He glanced at the girl's bowed head, knew he could make but one decision.

"Can't promise anything," he said, his voice bluff, "but I'll see what I can maybe work out. Meantime, if you've got a little grub, I could sure stand a meal. Been some time since I ate."

She spun to him, her eyes coming alive. "You think there is something you can do?"

"Hard to say. A wagon wheel is something a man just can't make up out of nothing. Maybe I can figure up a way to move."

"Oh, thank you!" she cried, her face shining. "Thank you, Mr. Campion —"

"Matt," he muttered.

"Thank you, Matt!" She stood on tiptoe, kissed him lightly on the cheek, then whirled away. "I'll fix you something to eat. Won't be much — and there's no water for coffee —"

"Anything will do," he said.

He stood for a time, staring at the wagon. He had tried not to commit himself, endeavored not to build her hopes too high, but now he was in it. Delay would be costly to him, could even mean his own life, not to mention that of Albert Toon. All he could do was move fast, keep the time loss to a minimum.

He moved to the side of the wagon, squatted down in its shadow. As he had known from the beginning, to repair the wheel was out of the question. Somewhere back along the way the iron tire had come off, become lost without their realizing it. Even if they recovered it there was no way of making a felloe or procuring spokes. They could forget the wagon.

He explained that to Della a short time later as they sat down to a meal of corn cakes, bacon, and canned peaches.

"But my father isn't able to ride," she said.

"We'll rig up a drag, a travois some call it," he said, his voice faintly impatient. "I'll split one of the wagon-bed sides and stretch canvas in between. Man usually cuts himself a couple of saplings for poles but since there's none around, we'll make do with something else. One horse can pull it. You'll have to ride the other."

"We have one saddle, an old one —"

"Good. I'm short on time so we'd better start at it now. First thing is to get your father out of the wagon. We'll fix him a bed there on the other side of the fire."

Together they moved Joshua Stockton to the outside and made him comfortable on a pad of quilts and blankets. The man seemed much weaker to Campion, but he said nothing of it to Della. He simply set to work at a furious pace constructing the litter.

He rigged a harness on the better of the two horses and tested the arrangement for a short distance in the rapidly failing light. It would do. He brought it back and halted near where the stricken man lay.

"Won't be too comfortable but we'll be able to travel," he said to Stockton. "Reckon we're ready to load you on."

Della looked up quickly from her work. "Tonight? Can't we wait until morning? My father isn't in any condition to start now."

"Be no different in the morning," Campion said, his tone edgy. "Cooler at night, anyway."

"He's right, Della," Stockton said in his low, faltering way. "Easier for the horses, too. I'm ready any time."

Matt knelt down, lifted the man, blankets and all, and placed him onto the drag. The horse shied momentarily at the feel of the load but settled down after a bit.

"Strip of canvas above your head there is to keep off some of the dust," Campion said, pointing to the makeshift shield.

Stockton nodded weakly. His eyes had sunk even deeper into his skull and a glazed look had come into them. There was a slackness about his mouth. "I thank you, Matt," he murmured.

Campion moved off to where Della was cramming a few selected items from their possessions into a flour sack. In another she had the remainder of their food. Matt picked up the worn saddle that lay on the pile of belongings and carried it to the other horse, a small black. The animal wasn't much and he had no bottom but he was the only choice they had. By the time Matt was finished, Della was ready to go. She moved by him, remote and silent, carrying the old shotgun in her hands. He watched her thrust it into the boot and climb onto her horse.

"All right," she said; her voice, neither warm nor cold, conveyed nothing.

He gave her a brief, irritated look. He sought no gratitude, only understanding of his own critical problems. Then it came to him that she could not know why he was in so great a hurry; he had told her little of his troubles, only that he sought to overtake another rider who was somewhere ahead.

He shrugged and mounted the sorrel. He would continue to keep it to himself. There was no point in further burdening her. He reached down, gathered up the lead rope to the horse that pulled the drag.

"Let's go," he said, and moved out.

11

It was slow going. The ends of the drag bit deep into the loose, dry sand and the horse tired rapidly. Joshua Stockton seemed to weather the rough passage fairly well; only an occasional groan escaped his lips as the litter bounced over some particular obstacle in the trail. There was the possibility that he was beyond the point of actually knowing or feeling much of anything. Matt Campion was not certain, but he suspected strongly this was the case.

They traveled in silence. Della rode near her father's side, and Campion was conscious of the deep resentment that was building within her. But he honestly could see no advantage to delaying, to holding up their progress. It would mean little to Stockton, and the hour would soon come when they must rest the horses anyway. He deemed it wise to get as far along as possible before it became imperative to halt.

That point was not far off, Campion realized shortly after they began the trip. The sorrel, fortified by his meal of hay, aided by the coolness, started the march with firm step and high head. He weakened soon, showed signs of faltering. Only the absence of the blazing sun and brutal heat made it possible for him to keep going.

Campion sought to maintain a steady pace. His own weariness matched that of the sorrel and the Stockton horses, but the need and urgency to lose no time, to push on before the killer became lost to him, kept him grim and rigid in the saddle. Within him, a hard, thrusting anger simmered, and he protested silently the position in which he had been placed. But he kept it hidden, allowed none of it to become apparent to the girl or her father.

Della was doing nothing by her attitude to ease the irritation. She hung back continually, slowed the small cavalcade at every opportunity. She never once voiced her objections but she made it clear by her actions that she heartily disapproved of Campion's haste. It came to a head near nine o'clock that evening, soon after they had crossed a broad, shallow swale and pulled out onto a rocky tongue of land.

"We must stop!" she declared, wheeling in

104

beside Matt. "I insist! My father can't go any farther without rest. And the horses — you're killing them!"

Campion gave her harried, overwrought face a quick glance, saw she was close to hysteria. He pulled the sorrel to a halt. He still felt it made little difference to Joshua Stockton whether they moved or remained stationary; he was at that stage where all things were remote, and his mind and body were indifferent to outside influences. But there was no way Matt Campion could explain that to the girl.

Tight-lipped, he dropped from the saddle and strode to the horse that pulled the drag. He loosened the shafts and lowered them to the ground, thus relieving the animal of his burden and adding to Stockton's comfort. Della was quickly at her father's side, brushing at his flushed features with her handkerchief, talking to him in a low, soothing voice as though he were a child.

Campion saw to the horses. There was not much he could do for them. There was no water at all left, the last drops having gone to ease Stockton's burning throat, and the small amount of timothy hay they had brought along should be conserved for the following day. He gave them a handful each, nevertheless, and turned wearily away, his steps leaden, his shoulders aching and stiff. He saw Della sitting a short way from her father, her face turned toward the low hanging stars in the west.

"He's sleeping," she said as he hunched down beside her. "He's so tired, so completely worn out." She shivered slightly. "I'm cold. Can we have a fire?"

They were out in open country. He shook his head. "Best we don't. We won't be here long."

She wheeled to him angrily. "Is that the real reason? And this mad hurry to keep moving while it's cool — are you certain there isn't something else behind it? Something that has to do with that man I saw early this morning?"

Campion waited out a long minute, his instincts rebelling at the thought of baring his problems to her. But perhaps he should tell her. It might make things easier for all. "Partly," he said. "I'm trying to help you and keep on the trail of that rider. I'm after him — and I mean to catch up to him before he can get away."

The determined tone of his voice did not escape her. "To kill him?"

"No — not unless he forces me to. I've been blamed for some killings he did. He's the one chance I have to clear myself."

She said, "I see." A moment later she asked, "Are there men hunting you? I've noticed you looking back over your shoulder several times as though you thought there was someone on our trail."

"A U.S. marshal," he said. "And maybe a posse. I left the marshal trussed up back there in the brakes. He's been riding my shadow since I left a town called Harmony. Doubt if he can shake himself loose of the ropes I put on him but he's a smart man, and a good lawman. I won't bet against his getting it done. And, of course, there's always the chance somebody might come riding by and cut him free."

Her brow had drawn into a frown. "A U.S. marshal," she repeated. "But if the man you're after is the guilty one, why should the law want you?"

"To them I'm the guilty one," he said and then told her the entire story: his arrest, Jud Wooster's claim to have seen him, the escape — all of it. When he was finished she remained silent, her eyes again lost in the heavens. One of the horses blew noisily, and far back in the direction of the abandoned wagon a coyote barked, summoning other members of his clan to his discovery.

"Maybe it would be best if you rode on," she said finally. "We're holding you back.

We'll make out somehow."

"Doubt it," Campion said, shaking his head. "I gave that some thought at the start and reckoned I'd better stay. Mean country to have trouble in."

"We'll be all right, now that we have a means to travel."

Only you'd be alone, Campion thought, still reluctant to tell Della Stockton her father would be dead before many more hours; that, indeed, he likely would not survive the night. And there was nothing anyone could do about it. In all probability the mark had been on him even before they pulled out from California.

"I'll stick," he said kindly, but in a firm voice.

"But we can't go on at such a hard pace! My father isn't up to it. And the horses —"

"They'll make it. They can take more punishment than you think."

Her head came up abruptly and her mouth set itself in a stubborn line. "Well, we aren't going any farther this night! We're staying right here. You can ride on if you wish."

Campion was suddenly angry. "Don't fight me!" he said in a taut voice. "I know what's best for you — for all of us. It won't hurt your father any to keep moving. Doubt if he knows what's going on. And the more desert we can put behind us while it's cool, the better off we'll be."

"That's just an excuse! You're anxious to keep going so you can catch that man you're chasing — or escape from that lawman who's following you. I don't know which it is, but I'm not going to let you make us a party to your scheme."

"Scheme!" Campion snarled. "I've got no scheme except to get you to some place where I can dump you, get you off my hands and conscience. A ranch, a town, another traveler — it doesn't matter which. Then I can go on about my own business, but until then I'm saddled with you and your troubles."

"Get rid of us!" Della echoed. "You're rid of us right now! We won't go another step with you."

His anger cooled at the desperate note in her voice. "Understand me a little. If I don't catch that killer, my life won't be worth a pound of dust. I'm good as dead."

"I understand well enough," she said bitterly. "And I realize that you're forcing us to go along with you at all costs, at the risk of my father's life."

The answer to that sprang to Matt Campion's lips, died there. The coyote far back on the desert lifted his wail to the sky again, ceased abruptly as though from cause. Campion's interest centered on that for several moments; it could mean nothing, or it could be a warning. Any number of things could have frightened the animal, caused it to hush.

"We'll move on together," he said quietly, getting to his feet. "And now." He glanced at the sleeping Joshua Stockton and then out across the almost flat desert that lay bathed in silver starlight ahead of them. "Looks smooth. Maybe he won't even wake up."

Della rose, walked off toward the horses. Matt turned to the sick man, lifted the drag and hooked it into the harness. Stockton groaned faintly.

"Get away from him!"

The girl's voice was sharp. Campion wheeled, exasperation a slow, burning fuse inside him. She was standing an arm's length away, the old single-barreled shotgun in her hands.

"We're not going with you," she stated, her voice trembling with emotion. "Get on your horse and ride out. I'm staying here until my father is able to travel."

Campion clung to his surging anger. "Don't be a fool!" he snapped.

110

"I'd be a fool if I let you use us — and that's what you're doing. You're making us a part of something, of the trouble you've got yourself into — and I won't have it! I won't let you drag us into —"

"Appears to me it's the other way around," Matt said wearily. "Put down that scatter-gun and get on your horse."

He moved off, placed his back to her. He heard a dry, ominous clack as she drew back the hammer of the weapon. He spun, swift as light. His arm shot out. His fingers closed about the tubular barrel of the gun, and he jerked hard, wrenching it from her grasp. A cry escaped her lips as she stumbled forward, off balance, and came up against him.

He caught her with his free arm, held her tight to prevent her falling. A great sob burst from her lips as she buried her face against his chest. For a brief time she remained in that position, held close in the circle of his arm; then she sprang back as if suddenly aware of what she was doing.

"You — you — heartless —" she cried, the words stumbling from her.

Campion stared, shook his head wearily, and stalked off. He broke the shotgun, plucked the shell from the chamber and hurled it off into the desert. He walked to her horse, jammed the gun into the boot, and continued on to where the sorrel stood.

He swung to the saddle, leaned down and took the lead rope of the drag horse into his hand. Only then did he look at her. She had not moved.

"Mount up," he ordered in a flat, uncompromising voice. "We're heading out."

He did not wait to see if she complied but put the sorrel into motion. When he glanced back several minutes later she was following.

12

Toward the morning, as they plodded wearily across the starlit flats, Matt Campion saw a darker smudge on the horizon. He watched it closely and, as they drew nearer, he saw it was a small oasis of rock and brush with a scatter of stunted trees lifting their pasteboard silhouettes against the sky. His spirits rose slightly with the discovery, for generally such places sprang into being around the infrequent water holes that appeared in the country.

Saying nothing to Della, he began to veer their course slightly westward. She noted the change and soon discovered the cause. She kneed the black she was riding up to his side and spoke for the first time since they had come to odds.

"Those trees — won't they mean water?"

"Maybe," he replied, unwilling to build her hopes too high. "Sometimes they don't."

As they drew nearer and the horses

showed no particular interest, he knew he was right. The spring would be dry. He made no comment to her but she saw it on his face, and despair once again settled in her eyes.

They pulled into the shadowy outbreak and halted. Della dismounted immediately and went to her father's side. Campion, looking first to the horses, made them as comfortable as possible and then sought out the sandy basin in the center of the shrubbery and rock. He dropped to his knees, began to dig into the hollow. The ground was hard and, with little hope of success, he located a sharp stick, probed deeper. Finally he gave it up. The spring had not seen water for months. . . .

He returned to where Stockton lay. Della looked up hopefully at his approach. He shook his head. Her shoulders dropped and she resumed her task of sponging her father's glistening forehead, doing it with gentle dabs of her handkerchief. Stockton brought his feverish eyes about and fastened them upon Campion.

"I fear we've put you to considerable trouble," he said in his halting, cultured voice.

Campion glanced across to the girl. Her lovely features were quiet, her eyes upon her parent. There was a deep sadness upon her and Matt wondered if she knew the end was near.

"Forget it," he said. "Both headed the same way. Glad I could help."

Stockton managed a tired smile. "Like my daughter, you're a poor liar." He turned his head, brought his attention back to Della. "I would like a few words with Matt, dear — alone."

She rose obediently and walked off toward the horses. She sat down on one of the larger, flat rocks, her face to the east, now beginning to lighten slowly.

"Like to see another sunrise," Stockton murmured wistfully. "But I'm afraid I shall be denied that privilege."

"Maybe not," Campion said. "Won't be long. Couple hours at most."

"A lifetime, perhaps," Stockton said. "Strange how precious every minute has become to me in these last few days. I have stored them up, hoarded them, like some sort of miser."

He paused, swallowed hard and with some difficulty. "You won't be held back much longer, Matt. . . . I can promise you that. I've already thanked you once for helping us. . . . I do so again. . . . But I —"
His voice caught, trailed off into a wrack-

ing cough.

Campion bent down, peered anxiously into the man's slack face. Stockton opened his eyes, smiled weakly.

"It's all right. . . . Just for a moment there, that was all. What I meant to say to you is that I'm afraid I am forced to ask another favor of you. . . ."

"Name it," Campion said.

"My daughter . . . Della . . . Please see that she gets started back to Ohio. We have relatives there. She knows who, and where they live. I have no money left to give her but take the horses. . . . Sell them and anything else I own. . . . Raise enough to buy her a ticket and pay expenses. . . ."

Campion said, "Sure. We'll manage it. You've got my word."

Stockton's features relaxed. "Thank you. It has been on my mind, a source of worry. I've wondered what would become of her because I've known this was coming . . . for months. . . . I hoped to reach Santa Fe before it happened. Friends there."

"Wouldn't it be better for her to go to them, instead of back to Ohio?"

The stricken man moved his head a little. "No, not now. This is no country for a lone woman — a girl. Better she returns to live with her relatives."

116

"However you want it," Campion said. "Reckon you'd better rest now. Hard day coming up."

Stockton smiled again. "Not for me, friend Campion. For you and Della, but not for me. And perhaps now it won't be so hard." He hesitated, added, "Matt, I hope you find the man you're searching for, that I haven't been the cause of your losing him."

"Forget it," Campion said, getting to his feet. He glanced toward Della. She was watching him, her face a pale oval in the half-light. He motioned for her and started to turn away.

"Matt —" Stockton's voice halted him. "Look after her — and thanks once more."

Campion said, "Sure," and moved off.

The chill had settled over the land and he built a small fire in the heart of the oasis, choosing a low place well surrounded by rocks and brush, where the glare of the flames would not be noticed from the surrounding desert. It would be a good thought to move Stockton in closer, he decided. Likely he was cold.

He glanced toward them, father and daughter. Della was on her knees, looking down at her parent. She was smiling. He was talking, telling her something that was amusing to her. Campion rose and went to the edge of the dead spring, to where he could no longer see them. He felt himself an intruder in those moments and he disliked being put in such position. He remained there until he heard a small sound by the fire and, turning, saw her standing there, her gaze lost in the small, dancing flames.

"He's sleeping," she said as he came up.

"Thought I'd move him in close to the fire. Wind's turned cold."

"He's all right," she said and stopped. Then, after a long minute, "He's dying, isn't he?"

Matt did not look at her. "One thing we all have to face someday."

Again she was silent. Campion knelt down, tossed a handful of dry sticks into the flames. "Sorry it had to be out here like this — at the end of nowhere. Seems like a man ought to have some comfort when he —"

"I think he prefers it this way. He always loved the desert. Can you tell me what he said to you?"

"Wasn't much. Only that he'd like for you to go back to your people in Ohio. I promised I'd see to it."

"He would be thinking of me," she murmured and began to cry softly. "That's like him — always thinking of others, never himself."

Campion put his arm about her slim shoulders, drew her close. He held her against his chest, sought to comfort her. She clung to him, sobbing quietly.

"It's so unfair," she said. "He wants to live so badly. Life always meant so much to him. Everything about it, in it. People, animals, flowers — even the wild weeds that grew on the hill slopes. . . . All of it meant so much to him — but he can't have any of it! While others, who count for nothing, who take life so tightly and for granted, who care for nothing but themselves — go on living. It's all so unfair — so unequal. . . ."

Her voice rose gradually with the torrent of words that poured from her lips. Campion felt her begin to tremble against him. He held her tighter, tried his best to soothe her.

"Men like you — men who kill other men — who think nothing of life! You snuff it out without a moment's hesitation — a thing so precious as life, so dear to those who can't have it! It means nothing to you!"

Her voice lifted to a shriek. Campion caught her by the shoulders, shook her roughly. "Hush! You want to wake him?"

Her sobs died in her throat. She pulled

away, placed her back to him while she wiped her eyes. After a minute, during which she regained her composure, she moved off, passed him by wordlessly, and went to Stockton's side. Matt watched her settle down beside the stricken man, saw her smile when he opened his eyes. Campion glanced toward the east. The gray streaks had turned now to a broad fan of brilliant orange and yellow, shot through with lances of purple and blue.

It would not be long before the night was gone. Joshua Stockton would have his last wish: he would see the sunrise once more.

13

Joshua Stockton died with his eyes on the rising flame in the east, his hand gripped tightly about that of his daughter. There was no smile on his thin, wasted lips, or any expression of pain. There was only a sort of lonely regret, as though he hated to begin the long journey into darkness without having first seen all there was of the light.

When it was done with, Matt Campion gently but firmly took Della to the edge of the brush and there sat her down where she could be alone while he made the necessary preparations. A suitable grave was difficult. He had nothing with which to dig and the harsh heat had baked deep into the rocky earth. But he worked steadily at it with a feverish impatience and eventually he had a shallow trench hollowed out. Wrapping Stockton in his blankets and the canvas that had served as part of the litter, he buried him.

Not until he was finished with a large mound of stones piled high as precaution against the animals, did he go for Della. He left her there beside the grave while he saw to the horses.

The full impact of his weariness hit Campion at that moment. The days and nights in the saddle with little food and almost no water; sleep gained only while astride the sorrel — the worry, tension, and plain manual labor involved in caring for Joshua Stockton, both alive and dead, struck him all at once.

He stood beside the gelding, sagged weakly against the nearly spent animal, and wished the chore would soon come to a conclusion. But there was little likelihood of that occurring. He had lost time with the Stocktons, and now he was pledged to further delay — seeing Della safely on. The horses could do little better than they had. Given fresh mounts, or the wherewithal to feed and water the animals they had, he could pick up the pace and regain some of the lost ground. But there was no possibility of that.

He struggled to organize his thoughts, get his fagged mind to function properly. The thing to do was to continue north, push on just as they had been doing and reach the settlement he had been told was there. It could not be too far distant now. A day, perhaps two. He had lost all sense of time and miles. Once arrived, he could arrange for Della's passage east. There would be stagecoaches running out of the town, he was sure. He'd manage to raise sufficient money somehow.

Once that responsibility was off his hands he would start again and search out the killer. Perhaps he would still be in the town, but most likely he had ridden on. A man weighted down with murder and several thousand stolen dollars would not tarry long in any one place. And if he had ridden on, there would be nothing to do but take up the trail again.

He wondered about Albert Toon. Was he still a prisoner in the brakes, or had he somehow gained his freedom? Were he asked to wager on it, his money would be on the latter. Toon was that sort of man — a good man despite his calling. Matt decided he would take no chances on it, however; as soon as he was on safe footing he would send someone back from the settlement to release the lawman.

He heard a small sound and came about slowly. Della Stockton stood before him. Her face was drawn and serious, her eyes deep and filled with shadows. She had her back to the sun and her hair was like a bright, golden halo about her head.

"I want to say something," she said, spacing her words distinctly. "I want to free you of your promise."

Campion shrugged. "Not for you to do. My word was to your father, I'll keep it."

She shook her head. "No — I refuse any more help from you. It was something you had to give — that you didn't give freely and willingly. And in the end it hindered you — and killed my father. It would have been better if I hadn't stopped you, forced you to help."

Raw anger, close to the surface, flared through Campion. "I didn't complain! And as for causing your father's death —"

"You did!" she cried. "You did! Your insistence that we hurry on, that we keep moving and never resting, caused it. It was your fear of that lawman on your trail that killed him. I know it did! If we could have rested more —"

"Would have made no difference," Campion snapped. "Your father realized his time had come. He knew it even before you left California, but he kept hoping you could reach Santa Fe before it happened."

"And we would have," she broke in, "if it

124

hadn't been for you! If only you hadn't pushed us so hard!"

Campion shook his head. It was useless to argue with her. He pointed to her waiting horse.

"I'm not going through all this again. Mount up. I'll see you to that town and then you'll be shut of me. I promised your father I would do that much, and I aim to whether you like it or not."

She had calmed again. "And if I refuse to go?"

"You'll go," he said quietly. "Even if I have to put you on that horse and rope you to the saddle."

"You would never dare — and I won't go! That's final. You don't care about me, or your promise to my father. You're just using us —"

"Using you?" he echoed blankly. "How?"

"You think I believe that story you told me about that marshal? That you're innocent of those killings, that the marshal is wrong? A U.S. marshal doesn't make a mistake like that! You're using us to aid your escape from him. If he had caught up with us you would have claimed you were in our party, that you weren't the man he wanted. It's something like that, I know. The law wouldn't be after you if you hadn't done something wrong."

"You don't make sense," he said, baffled by her logic. "I'm trailing a man who's ahead of us —"

"Oh, yes — the mysterious man who's riding a sorrel horse just like yours! The man who did the killings."

"You saw him yourself."

"Yes — maybe I did. But he's probably a friend of yours. A man who was with you in the murder and robbery. And now you're trying to get together."

Campion wheeled stiffly, his face set, whiteness showing along the rigid line of his jaws. "Think what you want to. Makes no difference to me. We're moving out and getting into that town. Then you can —"

He stopped in mid-sentence. A man, tall, powerfully built, with a narrow, bearded face and hard-surfaced black eyes, had stepped from the brush into the clearing. He was dressed in worn range clothing badly in need of repair, and his bushy, dark hair was long and unkempt.

"Howdy, folks," he said cheerfully, his thick lips pulling into a wide grin. "Name is Reemer. Duff Reemer. Heard you talkin', figured I'd have me a look-see at what was goin' on. There somethin' wrong?"

Campion eyed the man coolly, wondered

how long he had been standing there in the shadows, how much of the conversation he had overheard. There was something about Reemer that aroused his suspicion and mistrust; perhaps it was the slyness in his small, close-set eyes, the faint twist to his mouth. Or he may have felt only a normal aversion to his vile appearance and the sour body odor that oozed from him.

"No," Campion said coldly. "Nothing wrong."

"Sure didn't sound much like that to me," Duff Reemer said affably. "I'd reckon the little lady here was doin' a right smart amount of objectin' to ridin' on with you. That right, little lady?"

Reemer's glittering eyes ran slowly over Della's lithe body, paused on her hair. She cringed slightly, then seemed to gather her courage.

"You live around here, Mr. Reemer?"

"Just plain old Duff to them I like, ma'am. Yes'm, my place ain't far. Few miles to the west."

"Could we get some water there — and maybe rest for a few days? That is, could I? Mr. Campion here is in a hurry to reach the next town."

Reemer paused momentarily. Then, "Sure, sure, you bet you can. Me and my family don't see visitors much and we'd be plumb pleasured to have you stay a spell."

"Your family?" Campion said, Della's suggestion fusing with one that was forming in his own mind. "How far west of here did you say your ranch was?"

"Like I done told you, it ain't far. And I reckon you won't think it's much of a ranch. We're just poor folk but you're welcome to what we got, vittles and such. Lookin' at them horses, I'd say they could stand a mite of feedin' and waterin', too."

Della turned to Matt. "I think we've found the answer to your problem. I'll go with Mr. Reemer and stay with him and his family a few days. You can ride on, do what you have to do. I'll come on to the town as soon as I've rested some."

Campion made no reply. It was a good solution. Alone he could travel fast — but he could not dispel the suspicion that clouded his mind.

"Now, if you're worryin' about it, mister," Duff Reemer said, "why'n't you just ride along with us, sort of look over my place and see for yourself that everythin' will be fine for the little lady? Once you ease your mind you can head on out for Frisco Springs or wherever it is you're in such a hurry to get to."

That was a better suggestion and it agreed with Campion's thinking. Della did need rest, along with water and decent food; and she needed the company of another woman. He could also get grub and water for himself and perhaps the loan of a fresh horse. When he was finished at the settlement, Frisco Springs Reemer had called it, he would come back for Della and complete his promise to Joshua Stockton.

"All right," he said. "We'll do it that way."

They could change their minds if Reemer's place didn't look inviting enough. And they wouldn't lose much time since the man had said it wasn't far.

"You all jus' foller me," Reemer said, turning about and starting off through the brush. "Left my horse a standin' back on t'other side. Weren't too sure what I'd be buckin' up against when I heard all that talkin'. Man can't be too careful, sometimes."

Campion stepped to Della's side, attempted to assist her in mounting. She ignored him, went to the saddle on her own, and moved after Reemer. Campion shrugged, swung onto the sorrel. Della was making it plain she no longer needed his help.

14

Duff Reemer had a full canteen of water which he passed around, and that relieved one of their prime needs immediately. The man seemed anxious to help and grateful that they were to be the guests of his family and himself for a time, but Matt Campion, for some obscure reason, could not bring himself to like Reemer. Della, on the other hand, treated him with a friendly graciousness despite his slovenly appearance and if she noted his furtive interest in her, she did not mind.

They rode due west for the better part of an hour and, when finally they entered the low hills and broke out onto a long, cactus-covered ridge, they looked down upon Duff Reemer's ranch. It was a poor scatter of sun-grayed, sagging shacks, little more than huts, grouped at the edge of a water hole. No one was in sight as they rode off the crown and started down the short slope that led into the hollow. Again Matt Campion had that disturbed feeling that all was not as it should be.

"Don't see any cattle," he said, letting his gaze sweep up and down the swale.

Duff Reemer grinned apologetically. "Ain't got but a few. Not as lucky as some folk hereabouts. What we got is feedin' lower down, I reckon."

Matt's eyes shifted to Della Stockton, touched her briefly. He could read the chagrin on her face, but she was trying hard to conceal it. She had expected something more, something better than this assemblage of ramshackle shanties. But she would never admit it. He knew her well enough by now to realize her pride would conceal her disappointment and seal her lips.

In the steadily rising heat they rode slowly into the yard. The horses, smelling the water bubbling from a spring somewhere in the heart of the brush and rocks and flowing in a bright sparkling path into a small pond, quickened their step, craned their necks forward eagerly.

Campion, unaccountably wary, allowed the sorrel to have his head. He glanced sharply at the rotting hulks of the huts; they were even more dilapidated than he had at first thought. He wondered how Reemer and his family were able to live in them at all. The horses came to a stop at the pool, and he heard Della speak.

"Where is your family, Mr. Reemer?"

" 'Round somewheres," Duff replied, grinning. Then, "Reckon that's them now."

Two men had appeared, one at either end of the row of shacks. One, a huge, grizzled, shabby, straw-haired man with a matted, filth-laden beard, who looked more animal than human, held a rifle in his crusted hands. The other, somewhat smaller but nonetheless disreputable and threatening, carried an old combination three-barreled rifle and shotgun. That they were related was immediately evident to Matt Campion; that both were simple-minded idiots was also apparent.

Campion's hand dropped quickly toward his pistol. Reemer, watching him narrowly, spoke up. "Now, I sure wouldn't be tryin' that, mister. My brothers there ain't got much sense but they'd sure know what you was thinkin' on doin'."

Reemer slid from his saddle, circled around behind the sorrel. Keeping well back, he reached forward, lifted Campion's weapon from its holster and thrust it into his belt.

"Step down, folks," he said, grinning

broadly. "We're to home."

Campion dismounted, turned to aid Della. Her face was chalk-white, and fear had turned her stiff and silent. From the opposite ends of the littered yard, Reemer's kin closed in, shambling along on worn, run-down boots, unnatural, oversized heads thrust forward wolfishly.

"Your — your family —" Della stammered. "You said —"

"This here's my family," Duff said, waving his hand at the two drooling imbeciles. "The big one we calls Buster. T'other one's Holum."

"But your wife — you said —"

"Ain't got no wife," Reemer said. "Never did have. Always been just me and my brothers, since Pa died. But I'm thinkin' right hard on changin' my mind, seein' you. Always did fancy red hair."

"You goin' to keep her, Duff?" Buster asked, his mouth gaping like a fish, eyes shining with overbright intensity. "She goin' to be your'n?"

"I'm thinkin' on it, Buster. . . ."

Horror blanched Della's features. Campion felt her recoil, draw back against him. She trembled violently and a small, frightened noise escaped her throat. Matt put his arm about her while a stream of disgust and anger rushed through him. He had walked blindly into this; worse, he had let the girl in for it. . . . He faced Duff Reemer.

"You touch this girl," he snarled, "and I'll kill you!"

Reemer laughed uproariously. His brothers stared at him for a moment, then also began to rock with laughter. They stopped abruptly and Holum lurched forward, the hammers of his ancient weapon drawn back.

"Let me blow his head off, Duff! Let me do it, Duff! Always was wantin' to hold this here old shotgun again a man's head and pull the trigger. Always was wantin' to see what it'd do. Can I do it now, Duff?"

"No!" Reemer yelled. He lunged in, slapped Holum hard across the face. "Ain't nobody killin' nobody! You understand that?"

Holum blinked his eyes. "Why can't I, Duff? You allus lets us —"

"Not this one. He's worth a lot of money. I heard them talkin'. They's a U.S. marshal chasin' him and if a U.S. marshal wants him, then I figure there'll be a big reward."

"A U.S. marshal?" Holum echoed, his mouth sagging.

"A lawman, a sheriff, only bigger. One that works for the whole United States gover'ment. I'm goin' after him, bring him back here and give this galoot to him. Then I aim to collect the reward and get us a lot of money."

Buster, silent as a cat for all his huge size, had eased in close to Campion and Della. He had never removed his eyes from the girl, seemed fascinated by her glowing hair.

"Can't I have her, Duff?" he mumbled, extending a filthy hand tentatively toward her. The stench from him was sickening. "Can't I, Duff?"

"No!" Holum shrilled suddenly, abandoning his hopes of killing Campion. "It's my turn! You give that little Mex girl to him first, Duff. This'n is mine!"

"Get back!" Reemer shouted, stepping in between Della and his brothers. He raised his arm threateningly. "I told you, I'm keepin' her myself. You'd a still had that little Mex girl if you hadn't gone and busted her around so much. You stay away from my red-hair."

Buster reached for Della's arm, his senseless face ruddy and sweat-plastered in the harsh sunlight. "I could sure have me a time —"

Campion struck out savagely, knocked the man's hand away. Duff wheeled on his brother. "You hear me? You keep away or I'll bust you with a club!"

"I'm goin' to take me this here gal," Buster mumbled, wholly unaware of the warning, "and have me —"

Duff sprang forward. He swung a horny, balled fist, bringing it up from his knees. It caught Buster on the side of his massive head. Buster went backwards a half a dozen steps, sat down hard. The dull, animal expression never faded from his face. Holum broke out in a shrill peal of laughter, began to dance about hysterically.

"You hear me, Buster?" Duff demanded, rushing in. He drew back his booted foot, drove the pointed toe into his brother's ribs. "You leave her alone!"

Campion, watching through narrowed eyes, fought desperately for an idea, for a way out. He must get Della beyond reach of the Reemers somehow — at any cost to himself. Buster and Holum were insane, dangerous maniacs, and Duff was only a shade above his two brothers.

He kept his arm about Della, let his glance swing from Duff and Buster to Holum. The smallest of the three Reemers was standing only a dozen paces away. He had ceased his idiotic laughing and dancing, now stared with stupid, empty eyes at the prostrate Buster. He still held the three-barreled weapon in his hand, and now, again, it was pointed at Campion. Matt considered the possibility of lunging at Holum, seizing the weapon. It would be too long a chance; it could go off, and Della would be in the line of fire.

"Now you hear me good!" Duff shouted, reaching down for Buster's arm and helping him to his feet. "I'm lightin' out after that lawman. Don't you do nothin' while I'm gone except keep a watch on them two. You understand? I don't want you touchin' either one of 'em. I don't figure on havin' to explain nothin' to that marshal when I bring him back. You hear me, Buster?"

Buster nodded woodenly, his shaggy yellow hair jiggling with the motion of his head. An oily moisture still clothed his face and sweat trickled down his neck onto his hairy chest. His mouth hung agape and his vacant stare was again fastened upon Della.

"You, Holum — you hear me?"

"Sure, I hear you, Duff. I hear you good. We got to wait 'til you come back, then we'll have us a dancin' show."

"That's right. Just keep them here but don't do nothin' to them. Don't touch them." Reemer came back to Buster. "You take the man over there and put him in the tool shed. Bar the door. You hear — bar the door!"

"Can I take the gal somewheres, Duff?" Holum yelled, surging forward eagerly.

"I'm puttin' her in the house," Reemer said, waving Holum back. "Figure she'll be better off there. You all stay outside. Watch the door — but don't neither of you go in. Understand?"

"Sure, Duff. You want we should stay outside and watch the door, keep her inside 'til you come back."

"That's right, Holum. You boys are understandin' things real good."

Reemer turned his sly face to Della and Campion. "Ain't enough sense between the two of them to pour water in a bucket, but they'll mind what I tell them, so don't be gettin' no ideas. Long as you stay put you'll be all right, but you try runnin' and you'll get them all worked up. No tellin' what they'd do then, 'specially to a woman."

Hot words flooded to Matt Campion's lips, but he held them back. He was fighting to remain cool, to reason logically. Let Duff Reemer leave. The odds would even a little then. Once he was out of the way it would be easier to plan and execute an escape.

"Now you, mister," Duff said, grinning at Campion. "You trot along there with Buster. Don't be givin' him no arguments. I'm warnin' you — he can be real ugly when he

138

gets riled."

He reached out, took Della by the arm, jerked her toward himself. "Come on, little lady. You're goin' to the house and set nice and quiet 'til I get back."

Della, stricken dumb by shock, by fear, by the swift turn of events and the horror of her situation, suddenly found her voice.

"I won't!" she screamed, and jerked free of Duff's clawing fingers.

All Matt Campion's sane and careful reasoning, his determination to sit tight, to wait for a more opportune moment before he acted, exploded into thin air at Della's desolate cry. A wild fury roared through him. He lunged at Duff, drove his fist into the man's face, sent him sprawling to the ground.

"Get to the horses!" he yelled to Della and spun to face Buster, standing flat-footed and unmoving, his slow brain unable to grasp the sudden action. If he could seize the rifle, wrench it from Buster's hands, he would have a weapon to fight with.

He heard an eerie, nerve-shattering yell behind him. Holum! Too late he remembered, tried to dodge to one side. Something solid and heavy crashed against the back of his head. The world erupted in a shower of lights and then all was dark.

15

Stifling heat prodded Campion back to consciousness.

He was inside a small shed, one little larger than a wagon bed. Light streamed in through cracks in the roof and sides, and there was no window. He was soaked with sweat and his clothing, covered with dirt, was plastered to his steaming body.

He stirred, hearing the sound of voices somewhere outside his sweltering prison. Pain instantly shot down his neck, through his long frame. His head seemed to be filled with a thousand tiny sledge hammers, all thudding relentlessly at his brain. He sat up, fought back a wave of nausea and struggled to his feet. He reached out, placed one hand palm flat against the wall of his cell, and steadied himself. How long he had been out he had no idea; not for any great length of time, he guessed, for it was still morning. He could see the sun through the openings in the roof and it had not yet touched the mid-sky point.

He brushed at his streaming face, removed the sweat from his eyes. He saw the door directly before him and tested it quietly. It had been secured, probably with a drop bar across the outside.

He put his eye to one of the larger cracks in the wall, endeavored to locate the voices he had heard. It was Buster and Holum. They sat in the yard, in the full, blistering blast of the sun, seemingly unconscious of the searing heat. Small swirls of dust whipped about them as a low wind moved restlessly about. Beyond them Campion could see the horses. Having slaked their thirst, they had drifted into the maze of rock and brush where they now grazed indifferently.

There was no sign of Della and he supposed she would still be inside the house where Duff Reemer had deposited her — or had said he would. Buster and Holum were keeping the watch as they had been instructed to do. Matt wondered how long Duff had been gone. He would find Albert Toon, if he rode far enough. He could even encounter the lawman sooner, if Toon, by some means or chance, had gotten free of his bonds.

In any event there was no time to lose. He must find a way out of the shed, manage somehow to get Della to the horses, and escape. It would take some doing. Holum and his hulking brother had taken up positions almost squarely in the center of the yard. From there they could watch both the house and the shed with ease.

Campion listened to their disjointed run of conversation. They spoke of Duff, of what they would do when he got a huge bag of gold money for their prisoner. New saddles for all . . . a new shotgun . . . pistols . . . a whole barrel of drinking liquor . . . maybe some store-bought clothes. . . .

Matt moved back deeper into his furnace-like jail. His head throbbed dully and persistently from the blow Holum had dealt him, but there was no time to think of that now, or of the weariness dragging at him, or the gnawing hunger that clamored within him. Those things must wait. Duff could return at any moment, or he could be gone the rest of the day and all the night. Just which was problematical, and if they were to attempt an escape, they must do it soon.

A mounting fear for Della's safety was beginning to haunt him. He had absolutely no faith in the reliability of Buster and

Holum. After the hours wore on there was little likelihood they would remember Duff's warning and stay clear of the girl. Their animal lusts and appetites would eventually overcome their recollection and fear of his threats.

There were several worn and broken tools in the shed. A shovel with a splintered handle, a pick with half the head gone, a plowshare, rusty and badly nicked by rocks; a rake, a broken lantern, an axe handle. The glimmer of an idea came to Matt Campion. If he could draw the brothers' attention, get them near enough for him to use the axe handle as a club . . .

"I'm tellin' Duff!" Holum's frantic voice screeched through the quiet. "I'm tellin' Duff what you said!"

The sharp, meaty smack of a fist against flesh reached Campion. He stepped to the front of the shed, put his eyes to a narrow opening. Holum and Buster were wrestling about in the dust, flailing at each other wildly. Some sort of argument had erupted between them and brought them to blows.

They struggled furiously in the burning sunlight, cussing, screaming, biting, lashing out with fists and feet. And then abruptly it was over. Buster, after sitting astride Holum's prostrate body, rose. He drew back a few paces nearer the shed, breathing heavily, and glared at his dust-caked brother.

"You goin' to be tellin'?"

Holum whimpered. "I ain't sayin' nothin', Buster. I surely ain't! Only she'll be tellin' Duff herself and then he'll be mad at us."

"She won't tell," Buster declared. "I'll make her afraid. I'll bust her less'n she promises. Anyway, we won't be hurtin' her none. We jus' aimin' to look."

Holum sat up, mopped at his dirt-covered face with a sweaty forearm. "You sure enough goin' to strip her, Buster?"

"Sure 'nough. Goin' to make her dance for us. Ain't never seen no red-hair dancin'."

"That little Mex gal, she had real black hair and she danced good. You hadn't ought've busted her 'round like you done."

"She was mine, weren't she? Duff give her to me, didn't he?"

"Yeh, but after you done that she couldn't dance no more. You goin' to bust this here red-hair if Duff gives her to us?"

Buster wagged his head. "Ain't sayin'. Right now I'm just a thinkin' how she's goin' to look in there a twistin' and a turnin' and a jumpin' around. My — all that purty red hair! Like an antelope all streaked out and runnin' fast in the sun!"

"You recollect that ol' mule we tied up and skinned that day, Buster? You recollect how nekkid he looked, layin' there with no hide on. Bet she'll look just the same, all white like —"

"Bet she better not be doin' all the squallin' that old mule done!"

Holum scrambled to his feet, eyes glistening. "When we goin' to start, Buster? I'm a gettin' all fired up just thinkin' about it."

Buster wiped at his wet lips. "Reckon we'll just start right now. Come on."

They turned, shambled off across the yard. All the persistent tags of worry surged upward within Matt Campion and crystallized into a wild burst of fear. He threw himself blindly against the door of the shed. The tough, two-inch planks creaked but held firm, sending him reeling back onto his heels. Outside he heard Holum yell.

"Hey! That there feller in the shed's a cuttin' up, tryin' to get out. Reckon we ought to bust him good again?"

"Naw," Buster's answer came. "He ain't goin' to be gettin' out. Anyway, we ain't got no time now for him."

"But Duff said we was to —"

"You goin' to start in on me about Duff again? You want me to bust you?"

"No, only Duff —"

"You be shuttin' your mouth, Holum! If'n you don't, I'll make you stay outside and you won't be gettin' no chance for lookin' when —"

The slam of a door cut off Buster's final words. Campion, fear now a towering force within him, pulled himself to his feet. He hurled himself at the door again, recoiled from the sickening impact. He would never break out at that point.

He wheeled, seized the broken pick. There was no floor in the shed, no foundation. The upright planks had merely been sunk into the ground. He began to dig frantically. If he could hollow out a space large enough to permit him to worm under . . . Too slow. . . . And the ground was hard as iron. He drove the point of the pick under the edge of one plank, pried. That side of the shed creaked, lifted a fraction of an inch.

Encouraged, he yanked the pick free, tried a different board, one a little to the left. Again the shed moved, loosened. Working feverishly, he went entirely around the small structure until he had pried each wall free of the packed earth along its base. That completed, he stood back, considered the most logical direction in which to topple the tool shed, the way that would offer the least resistance. Backwards, he decided.

There seemed to be a slight slope to that point.

He retreated until he was standing against the front of the structure, beside the door. He saw the lantern that he had kicked to one side. A faint dampness on the ground around it showed it still contained oil. He snatched it up quickly, shook it, as a new thought came into his mind. There wasn't much of the liquid remaining, but enough.

Holding the lantern in his hand so that it would not again spill, he resumed his position near the door. He had but one plan — to throw himself against the back wall of the shed, several times if necessary, until it toppled. It was his only hope of getting free.

At that moment he heard Della scream, a wild, hysterical shriek of fear. It chilled Matt Campion to the bone, raised the hair on the back of his neck. He took a deep breath, clamped his jaws shut, and lunged at the wall, aiming his shoulder as high as possible to gain all the advantages of leverage. He misjudged slightly and his head came into contact with the thick planks. He rebounded, stunned, went prone to the ground.

But he had accomplished his purpose. The shed had not entirely gone over but was now canted, its front and sides lifted far enough from the ground to permit his escape. He rolled out into the open yard hurriedly, the shattered lantern still in his hand. Della's fear-ridden voice lifted again at that moment, filling the hollow with a nerve-racking wail. Through it, Campion could hear Holum's wild, idiotic laughing and Buster's loud voice, demanding, ordering, threatening.

Matt leaped to his feet, raced toward the house. The three-barreled weapon Holum had carried stood propped against the corner beyond the door. He unscrewed the cap of the lantern's reservoir, tossed it aside. He reached the entrance, and, closing his ears to Della's cries, dashed the remainder of the oil on the cracked, wooden planks of the wall. The tinder-dry lumber soaked it in thirstily. He was taking a chance, he knew. The flames would be near the doorway, could conceivably close it off. But it was more important at that moment to attract Buster and Holum, to draw them out into the yard.

He struck a match to the boards. Flames leaped up instantly, hungrily, licked eagerly toward the low, overhanging roof.

"Fire!" he yelled, and lunged for the shotgun.

A startled shout came from inside the

house. Campion snatched up the weapon, whirled about. The sagging door flew open. Holum Reemer burst into view. In his hands he held the rifle Buster had carried earlier. He saw Campion at that moment and a screech broke from his flaring mouth. He brought up the rifle fast, fired quickly. The bullet smashed into the side of the house, only inches from Campion's head, and showering him with a myriad of sharp splinters.

Holum plunged on, tripped, fell full length. He rolled to his feet, nimble as a mountain cat, levering the rifle. He swung it to his shoulder, now taking careful aim. Campion pressed the forward trigger of the shotgun. The worn, louse action released both barrels, one only a fragment of time behind the other. The recoil slammed Campion against the wall but he saw the twin charges of buckshot catch Holum Reemer in the breast, lift him off the ground and hurl him backwards into a bloody heap.

Campion threw aside the now useless gun, sprinted for the doorway of the shack. The front was now a mass of seething, crackling flames. In a few moments the entrance would be blocked by a sheet of fire. Ignoring the danger of Buster's presence, still somewhere inside the structure, he plunged into the room. Della, one shoulder bare, her dress ripped, lay on the floor in a dead faint. Beyond her in a corner, like a frightened animal, crouched Buster. The glare of the leaping flames reflected on his oily face and in his round, empty eyes.

Campion bent swiftly, lifted the girl into his arms and wheeled for the door. He paused there, looked toward the sniveling Buster.

"Come on — get out! This whole place is going up."

He did not wait to see if Buster heard, but leaped through the crackling flames into the yard. He paused beside Holum, scooped up the rifle, and rushed on toward the horses, now nervous and shying away.

He placed Della on the ground, dashed a handful of water from the ditch into her face. He moved on, hastening to halt the sorrel. If the horses, frightened by the fire, bolted, fled into the desert . . . But he caught the big red's reins, halted him. A long step away was Della's black. He tried to trot off, but Campion, acting with desperate speed, was too quick for him. With the leathers of the two mounts in his hand, he spun and hurried back to where he had left Della.

The water had revived her. She was getting to her feet, still somewhat dazed. "Got to get out of here!" he yelled above the roaring flames.

She nodded her understanding and he helped her onto the saddle. He vaulted onto the sorrel and they whirled out of the yard, Della clinging tightly to the horn. When they reached the edge of the clearing and broke out onto the desert Buster Reemer began to scream, his cries a weird, inhuman sound that came from the depths of the fire.

16

It had taken Albert Toon a full day to free himself. He had set to work with his teeth at the ropes that bound his wrists immediately after Matt Campion had ridden off. It had been a slow, painful process but eventually he released himself and took up the trail.

It was not a difficult one to follow, nor was it hard to decipher what had occurred when Campion came upon a wagon. Someone in trouble — and he had stopped to help. Campion was a fool. Not only had he permitted himself to become burdened and therefore impeded to a considerable degree, but he was also maintaining a strict northerly course, never once deviating. A smart man would be trying to cover his tracks, feinting, doubling back, doing all the fancy didoes that a man on the run always tried.

Of course, Toon realized, as far as Matt Campion knew, he was still in the brakes, helpless, tied hand and foot. He probably thought that no one was dogging his trail and he could therefore afford to be careless. That made Campion a bigger fool. A man should never take anything for granted; he should always be suspicious, watchful, even when he was sure he was in the clear. It was going to cost Campion his life. Horse, with his tremendous strength and staying power, was closing the gap between them fast; soon now Campion should be in sight.

In fact, he reckoned he better be taking a look at the country ahead. Wouldn't pay to blunder in too soon and scare off the pigeon. He pulled the paint off the trail, rode a short distance to halt beside the tangled branches of a mesquite tree. There was not enough to the sun-scorched shrub to really hide a man and horse, but it would serve to screen them from any casual search. A rider would loom up like a sore thumb on the open desert.

He stepped from the saddle, grunting as his heels hit the ground. He turned to his saddlebags and removed the field glasses. Edging around to the side of the bush, he put his attention on the north. His eyes picked up a small island of brush and rock, complete with stunted trees. A water hole.

The lawman sighed. Campion and his

party would have paused there, spent some time refreshing themselves. They would have rested and watered their horses and perhaps prepared some food. But they had not cooked anything, or even made coffee, for there had been no smoke in the sky. He amended that conclusion immediately. Campion might be more cautious than he had figured; he could have done his fire building while it was dark, killed it when daylight came.

He lowered the glasses, studied their round, metal eyepieces thoughtfully. Was Campion farther ahead than he had estimated? He had figured the man would be close now, little more than an hour in the lead. Traveling slow, and halting to rest, Toon had considered him almost within grasp. Now . . .

Toon lifted the glasses again. He should be able to pick up a dust cloud, some sign of the drag. It would be to the north, beyond the water hole. The lawman came to sudden attention. A rider had appeared a mile or so this side of the trees and brush. He had been down in a hollow, hidden from view; now he was coming back to the level of the surrounding desert.

Toon watched the man for a full five minutes. It was not Matt Campion, he saw

154

finally. It was a heavier person and he was not riding a sorrel horse. He was pointed due south and appeared to be following, generally, the trail Campion and his party had made. Probably it meant nothing, Toon concluded. The man was simply riding in that direction and, noticing the parallel grooves the litter had created, was using them as a marker.

He watched the rider draw abreast at a distance of a half a mile or so to his left, gave his rough features a cursory glance, and saw him pass on. Only then did he move back to the paint. Methodically he wrapped the glasses in their soft cloth and returned them to their customary place in the corner of the saddlebags.

He went to the paint's broad back, reined him out and away from the mesquite, and pointed his long head toward the distant water hole. Horse settled down to his steady, placid gait, as alike in nature to his impassive master as two living but dissimilar animals could be.

"We catch him soon now, Horse," Albert Toon murmured, indulging himself in one of his infrequent moments of optimism. "Pretty soon he iss our prisoner. Then we go home."

■ ■ ■ ■

The man Toon had seen riding south was Duff Reemer, and the stolid old lawman's desire to remain unnoticed was unfortunate for both of them.

Reemer was following the marks made by the drag, figuring that in so doing he would eventually run into the marshal. He rode on in the hot, driving sunlight, impervious to its withering touch, a man long accustomed to its blast and all the other hardships with which life had seen fit to plague him.

In his mind he was reveling in the good fortune that suddenly was his. There would be a big reward for Campion. No U.S. marshal would trouble to hunt down a man unless he was a big, important outlaw and badly wanted. Why — they might even pay a thousand dollars for him! And, on top of that, he was going to have a red-haired girl for himself. It was unbelievable he could be so lucky.

And about time. He had been saddled with his two brother all his life, it seemed. At first he hadn't thought it so bad, not when Pa was alive. He couldn't recollect much about Ma. She died while he was still a button, no more than knee-high. She had been a small, thin woman with long, stringy hair and odd, panther eyes. Once Pa had said she wasn't quite right. Maybe that was why Buster and Holum were the way they were.

While he was growing up Pa had looked after the pair and he hadn't paid much attention to them. Then Pa had died and he'd found himself with them on his hands, along with the old family place, which sure wasn't much, no matter how you looked at it.

From then on it had been a matter of survival for them by any and all means available, with the burden mostly on him. They grew a few vegetables in the garden below the spring but the ground didn't have much life in it and things didn't do very good. Mostly it was a matter of depending for food on deer and antelope and an occasional beef stolen from some rancher's herd. What little money he came by was from the pelts of animals they were able to catch, or from the pockets of the drifters who occasionally wandered in off the desert. *Trespassers,* Pa had called them, who had no right to be there, and so they never left. Now and then he got a day's work or two at some ranch, but that wasn't very often.

If it had been possible, he would have moved into town, either Frisco Springs to the north or Harmony on southways. There he could have got a job working in a livery stable, or swamping at a saloon. He might even have got himself on as a shotgun guard for one of the stage lines, which was the best job any man could have. But leaving the old place and moving into a town was out of the question. Pa had always told him Holum and Buster couldn't be taken to live around regular folks. They had to be kept off to themselves.

That was all over with now. He'd been thinking on it all the way from the ranch. He was going to start doing something for himself. Once he collected the reward money, he'd take the red-haired girl and move on. Let Buster and Holum shift for themselves. Just wasn't right that he should spend the rest of his life looking after them. One of these days they were going to kill each other, anyway. It had almost happened the day he'd brought a young Mex girl home with him.

He'd found her walking across the desert, almost dead. The Apaches had caught her a few years back, she said. She got loose from them and was trying to get to the border where her folks were. He'd loaded her up behind him on the saddle and carried her home. She hadn't been there an hour when

Buster and Holum got to scrapping over her.

Buster almost beat the small Holum to death, likely would have if Duff hadn't been there to pull them apart. They were like a couple of wild dogs fighting over a bone. But anyway Buster had won out and the little Mex had become his private property. She lived three days and then they had to bury her. The grave was out there on the hill, along with Pa and Ma and the three, or was it four, drifters.

Duff Reemer swallowed hard, thinking of the red-haired girl waiting for him back at the house. She'd called him Mister Reemer and that was mighty high sounding. He reckoned that sort of showed she liked him. Hadn't exactly appeared that way to him at first but as he rode along, thinking on it, he realized what she meant. It was a real comforting thought, having a woman pretty as that red-hair for his own.

He wasn't going to treat her mean, bust her around like Buster did the little Mex girl. With the thousand dollars he was going to get he would take her and move into town so's they could live like regular folk. He'd buy her nice dresses and maybe get a buggy that had a top and side curtains to keep the wind and sun out. He'd get himself a job, maybe even a shotgun messenger's job. Everybody knew a shotgun messenger was an important man, one everybody figured was mighty big.

He reckoned he oughtn't to feel as he did about Buster and Holum. After all, they were his kin and Pa had hammered and hammered at him that it was his bounden duty to look after them. But a man can take so much; just because he was born with good sense was no reason he had to wear his life away wet-nursing a couple of half-wits. Just wasn't right to expect it of him.

He shifted suddenly on the saddle, slapped his leg violently. By God — he wasn't going to stand for it any longer! He'd collect his thousand dollars — maybe it would even be as much as two thousand — take his red-hair woman and high-tail it clean out of the country, just like he'd been figuring to do. He'd not stew and fret any more about it. Let Holum and Buster starve, if they didn't have any better sense. He was through looking after them.

A sudden thought lodged in his mind; maybe it was a mistake to leave his red-hair woman back there at the place. Maybe she wouldn't be safe with Buster and Holum. He'd warned them not to bother her, threatened them if they did. But sometimes they forgot, and when Buster took something into his head it was powerful hard to get it out. Blind fear gripped him by the throat. You reckon they might do something to her? By God, they'd better not! He'd kill them both!

And damn that U.S. marshal, too! Where was he? He should have showed up before now. He was a far piece from the ranch and if he kept going much longer he'd be riding down Harmony's main street! He twisted about on the saddle, threw his glance toward the north to calculate the distance he had come.

That was when he saw the thick smoke clouds boiling into the empty sky.

17

Campion pressed the pace until the horses began to falter, and then slowed them to a walk. Since there had been no way of knowing where Duff Reemer was at that moment of escape, he had deemed it wise simply to assume the man was nearby and act accordingly.

He glanced at Della, a length behind him. She had recovered from her faint and was riding the black with expert ability. She had managed to pull her torn dress together and now showed no effects from her harrowing experience with the Reemers, except in her eyes, which still glowed with a reflection of the fear that had gripped her. He slowed the sorrel, allowed her to draw abreast.

"You all right?" he asked.

"I'm all right," she answered crisply.

He grinned wryly at her show of disfavor, but said nothing. There been moments of sheer terror and horror for her back at the Reemer place, and he guessed she had good reason to be upset. But it was not finished with yet; there was still Duff to reckon with.

He turned to the trail again. They were following a course that ran along the edge of low-lying hills. It was some miles west of the route they had taken earlier that day, but Campion elected to stay with it. They would be less noticeable — both to Reemer and to Albert Toon, if he was on the prowl again. The longer Della and he could remain inconspicious, the safer they would be.

But the protective bulk of the hills did not shelter them for long. Near the middle of the afternoon, with the sun bearing down with all its strength and a hot wind out of the south stirring the dust and weeds vigorously, the mounds dissolved into one last rock-scabbed slope, and they were again on the flat, open desert.

"Matt —"

Campion turned in surprise at the sound of Della's voice. She was looking directly at him, her features strained in the cruel, intense sunlight.

"I want to tell you I'm sorry."

"Sorry?"

"For the way I acted and talked . . . like a

163

spoiled child. I — I almost got us both killed."

He made no immediate reply. Then, "Forget it. One thing I'd like to get straight with you, however. I won't say I've never gunned a man, but I didn't have anything to do with killing those two they're blaming me for."

"I believe you," she said simply. "I guess I did all along. It was just that I was so angry. I felt that you caused my father's death."

"You don't now?"

She said, "No. . . . Looking back I can see that it was coming, that probably nothing could have prevented it. Maybe I should blame myself. We should never have left California. And if I hadn't got us lost and we had been able to reach Santa Fe —"

"Still would have happened. Maybe not so soon. He might have had a week or two, but I doubt it."

She was silent as the horses plodded wearily along through the searing heat. She half-turned, looked back over her shoulder.

"It's hard to leave him back there — so far from everything — so lonely."

"I don't think he minded," Campion said, searching for words to comfort her. "I think he saw something in this country that the rest of us miss. A rare beauty, you might call it, a thing that goes deep and that few of us ever become aware of."

"He always loved the desert," she murmured. "Many times he spoke of it, said things like it being another world, a place where men were intruders and had no right to be."

He let her talk, knowing that it helped, that to unburden her heart and speak of her father was a way of cleansing the sorrow that lay so heavily upon her heart.

". . . I think if there had been some way to make a living, our home would have been on the desert — far out in the very center of it. But that was impossible. He was a teacher, you know. We had to live in the towns. It was hard enough just to get people to send their children to school, as it was. . . ."

Campion was only half listening. His eyes were on the sky, now a brassy haze. The air, stirred by fitful gusts, was heavy and smothering. Far off to the southeast monstrous, yellow clouds clung to the horizon. The heat had not lessened, seemed to have become more oppressive and demanded more of their strength. The horses moved at a slower, painful pace.

She saw that his attention had drifted. "What is it?" she asked, a note of fear creeping into her voice. "Is it Reemer — or that other man, that marshal?"

He shook his head. "Sandstorm blowing up. Bad one, looks like."

He swore silently to himself. More delay, more hindrance. They had been making fair time, actually doing pretty well since they had broken away from the Reemer place. And now this. It seemed all manner of things conspired to prevent his overtaking the man on the sorrel. It was almost as though it was intended for the killer to escape, that he should pay for a crime he did not commit.

"Can we miss it — avoid it somehow?"

Campion stirred impatiently. "Not a chance. Out here in the open we're caught flat-footed."

He was no stranger to the wild, sweeping upheavals that periodically scourge the desert and plains country with stinging clouds of sand and dust. From them there was no escape, no place to hide, no relief; all things simply came to a standstill and suffered out the minutes, or hours, or oven days until it was over.

They should attempt to locate some sort of shelter. A low hill was better than nothing at all. He raised himself in his stirrups, probed the land with squinted eyes. The line of hills they had followed after departing from Reemer's was beyond sight. It would be foolish to double back, endeavor to reach them. The storm, already a boiling, brown mist, was beginning to obscure the distance. It would catch them before they had gone a half a dozen miles. And to the left — Matt Campion grew rigid.

A rider had broken over a low roll in the land a thousand yards or so to the south. A big man on a big horse, coming up steadily. It could only be Toon, free and once again on the trail. If it were Reemer he would be showing up farther to the west. He swung his attention quickly to the opposite direction, hopeful that Della had not also noticed the horseman.

"There's a break in the flats on ahead. Maybe a mile," he said, thankful in many ways for that bit of good fortune. "I can see brush, and it could be an arroyo. We'll make for it."

It would not offer much in the way of shelter but it would be far better than getting caught out on the almost unbroken table of the desert where there was nothing at all to break the force of the wind and the slashing sand. And it would screen them from the prying eyes of Albert Toon.

They veered west, pointed directly for the smudge of brush. Campion prodded the horses for speed, hoping they could get out of sight quickly, before the lawman could spot them. The rising storm helped some, for dust clouds now were drifting across their trail. Once, when he cast a glance over his shoulder, he could barely see Toon. He was little more than a vague shadow in the yellow gloom.

With each passing minute the wind increased and by the time they reached the scatter of greasewood and mesquite, which grew, not in an arroyo, as Campion had at first thought, but in a fairly low swale, it was lifting to peak velocity. Great gusts of dust and stinging sand slapped at them, whipped them mercilessly, filled their eyes and mouths with gritty particles and choked their lungs until it was difficult to breathe.

They rode into the cup, with the sun a huge, blood-red disc behind the yellow pall. Immediately they no longer felt the direct whip of the wind, but the sand and dust swept in upon them in continuous clouds and there was no slackening of the stifling heat.

Campion dismounted, wheeled to help Della. Coughing and choking, she slipped to the ground, holding a hand over her mouth. Campion tied the sorrel and her black to a clump of brush nearby, making certain the knots were secure. The two horses immediately swung about, placed their rumps to the buffeting wind.

He returned to Della, took her by the hand and led her a short distance to where a half-buried ledge of rock formed a miniature butte. They sat down, crowded up close to it for protection. The wind was thus blocked, but the sand continued to filter down upon them in a solid curtain.

"Wait a minute," Campion said after a time, and rising, went to where the horses cowered in the howling blast. He jerked his blanket roll free of the saddle, struggled briefly with the gusts that threatened to tear it from his fingers, and returned to the ledge. Again fighting the force of the storm, he unrolled it, threw it over their heads as a canopy. By allowing it to hang behind their shoulders, and then leaning back against the rock, they were able to anchor it securely. Immediately conditions were much improved.

"How long will this last?" Della wondered after they had made themselves as comfortable as possible.

He shook his head. "Hard to guess." He was thinking, not of Albert Toon again dogging his trail, or of Duff Reemer likely somewhere out in that shifting world of sand and dust, searching, closing in — but of the man on the sorrel drawing farther away from him with each passing minute.

18

For Campion and Della Stockton, crouched beneath the low bluff, the night was endless. They dozed fitfully, a sleep induced by near exhaustion, but the wind, which raged and howled and tore at the flimsy cloth protecting them, permitted no real rest. Finally, with the coming of dawn, the storm slackened, faded to a low whisper, and finally died.

Choking and coughing, they rose. Campion went first to the horses. They had withstood the blasts fairly well and, after he had brushed the accumulated sand from their eyes and mouths, they began to move about in quest of grass. But the storm had covered the floor of the swale with several inches of fine sand and what little forage had grown there was now buried beyond reach.

Thirst was a nagging demon now, to man and beast alike. The hot wind had sucked them dry and there was no possibility of relief. Water had been plentiful at the Reemer place but there had been no time in which to fill the canteen, and Campion, turning his eyes to the north, realized they had no choice but to push on for the settlement.

He wondered about Albert Toon and Duff Reemer. Both would have halted for the storm, would now be up and moving on. Fortunately there would be no trail for them to follow; the drifting sand would have taken care of that. But Toon would guess their ultimate destination, as would Duff Reemer. And Reemer, acquainted with the country, would move fast. He scanned the horizon carefully. Neither man was in sight, but both were out there, somewhere.

He glanced at Della. She was wiping the dust from her face with a small square of lace-edged cloth, and striving to pin back her disarranged hair. He noted how it fell about her head in thick, bright folds, and for several moments he was caught up by the absolute beauty of it. She glanced up, saw that he watched her. She smiled lamely.

"I'm a mess," she murmured. "Wish I could do something about the way I look."

An awareness of the steady, relentless passage of time was upon him. "It's fine.

Expect we'd better get moving."

She continued to work with her hair and then suddenly she gave him her direct glance. "You wish I would hurry, don't you? It's dangerous to remain here."

He shrugged. "Matter of fact, it is what I'm thinking."

She gave the coppery coils a final pat. "There, it's the best I can do." She started toward the waiting black. "The storm — and our having to stop — has made things worse for you, hasn't it?"

"Nobody moved last night," he said, helping her to mount. "As for the man ahead, any guess is a good guess. He could still be in that town, or he could have gone on. Depends on a lot of things."

He mounted the sorrel and wheeled about, climbed the grade out of the swale.

"Wish we had water," she said. It was no complaint, merely a voiced desire.

The harsh fear that had gripped her during those hours after they left the Reemer place were entirely gone now. Either that or she was hiding it from him, unwilling to burden him further. The sorrel broke out onto the flat tableland again and Campion's eyes automatically made a swift circuit. It was an empty world, devoid of everything except the heat already beginning to hang in quivering layers. If Della was noticing thirst so early, by sundown —

He dismissed the thought, said, "May run across another water hole, one with a good spring this time. We're going to need food, too. I'll keep my eyes peeled for a rabbit or something we can eat."

She was beside him. "How far is it to Frisco Springs, do you know?"

"Ten miles, or a hundred. I'd say it's about half way between."

"Horses are in sad condition, too," she said, for no particular reason. "The poor beasts, they've had a hard time of it."

"Lucky they watered and grazed a bit yesterday. Otherwise we'd be walking now."

He took his directions from the sun, and they rode slowly off northward across the gradually warming desert. Della was light-hearted, almost gay, but he knew she was forcing herself, putting it on for his benefit. Several times he saw her look back, saw the worry touch her face and fill her eyes briefly. But she said nothing, continued to fill the passing minutes with conversation that dealt with her life in California, her father and the dreams that never came true for him; even with Campion and his plans for the future.

As the hours ground on and the terrible,

blistering heat once again enslaved the land, her words began to slow, and finally she fell entirely silent. Matt studied her from beneath the wide brim of his forward-tilted hat. It was unbelievable she could have withstood the grief and terror and hardships she had experienced in the past days and nights so well. Della Stockton was a woman any man could be proud of.

They rested the horses at midday beside a lone mesquite that grew off the point of a sandy ridge. There was no relief from the broiling sun, no particular reason to pause beside the thin, starved shrub, except that it was a break in the vast monotony of the endless plains.

Campion left the girl reclining on the hot sand and climbed to the crown of the ridge, only a few feet above the level of the desert. There he squatted on his heels and began a slow, methodic probing of the gray-and-brown sea that flowed about them, spending most of his efforts on their back trail. The knowledge that both Toon and Reemer were somewhere in the area was an ever tightening noose about his neck, slowly choking him with its pressure, wearing him down with its threat.

If he was going to be trapped he hoped it would be by Albert Toon. At least Della would then be safe. But if Reemer caught up with them first — he trembled, thinking of the fate that would befall her should Duff succeed in taking him unaware, and kill him. Duff was as mad as his two brothers except in a different, less apparent way.

"Are there any signs of them?"

Her halting question startled him, brought him about quickly. She had moved up the slope, unheard by him, and now gazed at him through clear, grave eyes.

"I know they are out there, Matt. Both of them. Don't try and keep it from me. I've seen you look around, study the country behind us a hundred times since we started this morning."

He grinned. "Appears we've both had the same idea."

"I don't see how they could hide. The desert is so flat, so empty."

"Fools you," he said. "Lot of low hollows. And the heat does funny things to your eyes."

"Then they could be close?"

"Possible. I saw Toon — the lawman I told you about — late yesterday, just before the storm hit. I don't think he saw us but I won't bet on it."

"And the other one — Duff Reemer?"

He shook his head. "No sign. Could be

he's not out there at all."

He hoped she would believe that; it would lessen the tension that he knew gripped her but that she was striving so bravely to hide. She was not so easily put aside.

"He's out there," she said quietly. "We both know it. He'll not rest until he avenges his brothers' deaths, and . . ."

She did not finish what she intended to say. He knew what it was, nevertheless. Duff Reemer had set his mind to have her, and to him that would be as important as his revenge.

"He's the one we've got to think about," Campion said, grudgingly admitting the danger. "He knows this country and will figure we headed north. If there's a way to cut in and get ahead of us, he'll take it."

Now that he knew she was fully aware of all their peril, Campion was relieved. He had thought to keep it from her only to spare her worry. Two pairs of eyes on the alert would be much better than one.

She rubbed at her throat, swallowed with difficulty. He bent down, picked up a small pebble and handed it to her. "Keep that in your mouth. It will help some."

She did as he directed. Then, "I never thought I would be thankful for a sand-storm, but I am. Could we have lost them?"

"Not much chance. Most likely they stopped, just like we did. And started up again when it was over. Our one hope is to keep in front of them, hold our lead and reach Frisco Springs before they catch up."

"Then we'd best move on," she said at once. "We've no time to lose."

Keeping low, he crawled back off the top of the ridge. He glanced at her critically. "You're about all in."

"I'll be all right," she said. "It's the horses I'm worried about. Hadn't we better walk some, lead them so as to save them as much as possible?"

Again Matt Campion marveled at the slim, red-haired girl who stood before him. "You've about got it figured. But when it gets too much for you, say so. In this sun you play out fast."

They left the mesquite tree, leading the worn sorrel and the black. Campion maintained a close watch on the girl, and when he saw her begin to falter he helped her onto her saddle and climbed aboard the gelding. From that time on it was an endless process of alternately walking and riding, a nightmare of tedious progress across the burning, endless desert.

Near the middle of the afternoon the black went down, spilling Della onto the hot sand. She staggered to her feet, unhurt, but it was the finish for her pony. Campion, feeling vaguely light-headed, removed the gear and threw it to one side. He should put the horse out of its misery, he realized, but he was reluctant to risk the sound of a shot. In the dead, silent heat it would carry for miles.

They moved on, wordless now under this new crisis. He walked continually now, forcing Della to ride the gelding at intervals. There was a strange, unaccountable weakness in his body, but he ignored it, pushed on, driven by the relentless pressure of their great danger, a merciless, irresistible force. The sun baked them dry, dehydrated them completely. Sweat no longer seeped from their bodies, and their clothing had turned stiff, and chafed their skins raw at every move.

Close to dark Campion saw the low, gray-green blur of a water hole, or perhaps it was only a thick stand of greasewood and mesquite collected in a swale. And possibly it was only his imagination, a mirage induced by the blinding, shimmering heat. He watched it for a long time, decided finally it was real, that it was shrubbery of some sort.

Whether it was a spring or not, it offered shelter from the sun, relief from the vast, unfriendly and barren desert. He called it to Della's attention, saw her eyes light up with hope. Somewhere in their tortured bodies they found a well of new strength and together they pushed forward eagerly.

Duff Reemer had paused only briefly in the smouldering shambles that once had been home to him. There was not a single thing standing. The fire had consumed every structure, even to the pole corral. He quickly found Holum, saw in a glance that he was stone dead. Buster, or what remained of him, he saw a few minutes later lying across the rock threshold that marked the entrance to the house. Evidently he had gotten trapped inside, sought escape, and failed.

Duff did not give them a second thought. They were better off dead. He was also better off with them both gone; he had intended to desert them anyway and this saved him the bother.

What did lift his anger to a furious pitch was that he was now out not only the reward money he had planned on so strongly, but the red-haired girl who rightfully belonged to him had been taken. This was something he just couldn't abide. For the first time in his life he had been given the opportunity to have something, to be someone — and it all had been snatched away just as he reached for it.

That Campion — that damned Campion! Blast his mean, thieving soul to hell!

He was at the bottom of it all. By tricking Buster and Holum he had managed to escape and when he did that, he just the same as threw Duff's reward money, at least two thousand dollars, into the quicksand. . . . To make it worse he had run off with the red-haired girl who was also Duff's property. He had set great store by that red-haired girl and it wasn't right that Campion should do the mean things he had.

Maybe all wasn't lost yet.

Campion would head north. He wouldn't try going south, not with a U.S. marshal on his trail. He would try to reach Frisco Springs so he could hide out with the girl. They couldn't travel very fast. Their horses were in bad shape. If he started right then and pushed hard he ought to be able to catch up before they got to the town.

He swung out of the yard, ignoring the bodies of his brothers, the steadily rising wind, and all else. He rode fast, following a direct line north. Near midnight he was forced to halt and pull in behind a stand of mesquite and thorn bush and get himself and his horse out of the wind's fierce blasts.

In the early morning, as soon as the storm was over, he was back in the saddle. His eyes were red; his face, a gray mask of sand and dust. His teeth gritted on the particles that had accumulated in his mouth, but none of this did he notice; one thing only possessed his brain — *Kill Campion.*

He drove his mount heartlessly through the day and its devastating heat. Once the faltering animal stumbled and they went down in a turmoil of boiling sand and dust, but Duff was on his feet quickly, cursing, dragging at the reins, pulling the horse upright. The visions of life with the red-haired girl and the reward money were like a spur at his flanks, and he never once lost sight of the rich and fulsome future that was to be his — when he overtook Campion.

Late in the afternoon, as he halted on a sandy ridge to stare across the glittering flats, the clean, distinct report of a rifle shot rolled in to him. His cracked lips parted in a gleeful grin. He knew now where Campion was, where he had taken the red-haired woman — his red-haired woman. His huge hand dropped to his side, reaching for the pistol that hung at his hip as he contemplated the joy of killing Campion. His fingers touched only the empty holster. The gun was gone — lost probably when his horse had stumbled! But it didn't matter. . . . It would be more pleasurable to kill Campion with his bare hands. . . . He could make it last longer. . . . Make Campion scream and suffer and beg for mercy. . . .

He thumped his heels into the sweaty sides of the horse with cruel force, sent him plunging down the slope at reckless speed. The water hole . . . That's where they were hiding. They had stayed farther west than he had figured. . . . Made no difference. He had found them and they weren't far away.

19

Campion killed the rabbit with a single, well-placed bullet. It had been crouched beneath the brush as they approached, watching them curiously as though disturbed at the sight of humans invading its domain.

Matt had hesitated again about using the rifle. The shot was almost certain to be heard by Toon and Duff Reemer. But the hunger that racked Della, as well as himself, overruled all precautions.

He gathered up their small prize and moved deeper into the oasis, leading the sorrel. Della, still in the saddle, was silent. He pointed for the center of the wild growth, to the low area where water should be flowing. He had felt certain the spring would be alive. The shrubbery here had a much greener, fresher tint than that at the other oasis. Disappointment hit him with the solidness of a hammer blow when he saw only dry sand.

He made no show of it before Della but halted, helped her to dismount. She remained where she stood, stricken wordless by defeat and the day's terrible punishment, and numbly watched while he led the sorrel off to one side where bunch grass spotted the ground.

He came back to the spring and for a time he simply stood and stared at the sand while his throat contracted spasmodically in its craving for moisture. He dropped to his knees, began to claw at the basin. There must be water — these had to be! He searched about for a sharp stick, located one of suitable length, and fell to digging again. He worked feverishly, using his cupped hands frequently to scoop out the loose particles and cast them aside.

Abruptly he sat back. A low, croaking sound escaped his lips. His fingers had touched moisture — there was no mistaking it! He flung a triumphant smile at Della, set to work now at rushing pace. He gouged the hole deeper and deeper. When he was down near two feet a muddy ooze began to seep into the pit.

"It's here," he mumbled. "Got to dig more. . . ."

He began to stab into the bottom of the

hole, driving the stick half its length into the muck. Water began to rise slowly, steadily. . . . Thick, silt-laden liquid to be sure, but that didn't matter. It would clear. He heard Della give a small cry, felt her touch against him as she dropped to his side.

"Water and food," she murmured in a grateful voice.

He grinned. It was so little to be thankful for — muddy, gritty water; a stringy jackrabbit — but it was food and drink and it would satisfy the cravings of their bodies.

He rose, removed the empty canteen from his saddle. He returned to the spring where Della had wet her handkerchief, was holding it to her parched lips while she sucked out the moisture. He took the square of cloth from her, held a single thickness over the mouth of the container and submerged it in the now almost completely filled hole.

"Strain out some of the dirt," he said.

When it was half full he removed the cloth and handed it to her. She took it eagerly, drank hurriedly. Gently he pulled it from her grasp, anxious that she should not drink too much, too fast. He tipped it to his lips, allowed the liquid to first slosh about in his mouth to relieve the dryness, and then trickle down his burning throat.

The gelding smelled the water, nickered anxiously. Campion refilled the canteen and got to his feet.

"This will do us for now," he said. "I'll see to getting that rabbit cooked if you'll water my horse. Not too much all at once."

The moisture entering their bodies had worked magic. Campion felt his strength and spirits rise almost immediately, saw an identical effect upon Della. He moved about through the brush and rocks, collecting dry sticks for the fire with renewed vigor. The girl, he noted, had managed to wash her face, was at that moment sponging off her hands and arms, again using the handkerchief.

He scooped out a place in the center of the oasis and started the fire. It was almost full dark and he didn't worry too much about the smoke. In another few minutes it would be invisible. After the flames were going strong, he rigged a spit, using two forked sticks and one straight one, and then set about dressing the rabbit. By the time Della had finished with the sorrel he had their meal on the fire, and the tantalizing aroma of roasting meat was filling the area.

Later, when they had picked clean the last of the rabbit's bones, they sat back knowing the comfort and contentment that only gnawing hunger and maddening thirst, finally satisfied, can bring.

"It was so little — yet so much," Della said dreamily.

Campion helped himself to another long drink. He sloshed the canteen. "At least we won't have to worry about water tomorrow," he said. "We can start out with this full."

"And your horse won't suffer so much either," she added. Her expression turned serious. "Would it be best to move on tonight, after a little rest, I mean? That rifle shot would have been heard."

"Have to gamble on it," he replied. "Sorrel's no shape now to head out — at least not for five or six hours. And he'll have it tough tomorrow, carrying double some of the time."

"I had almost forgotten," she said quickly. "It's bad isn't it, with just one horse?"

"Bad enough. Means a lot of walking."

"And slow going."

Slow going. He realized with a start what that meant to him. With Toon and Reemer snapping at their heels, and the fearful trials and tribulations of the past day and night, his need to hurry, to overtake the man on the sorrel, had faded from his mind. He shrugged, feeling the old irritation and resentment lift within him. He would have reached Frisco Springs by that hour, had he been left alone, had he not been sucked into someone else's troubles. And likely he would have been a free man again, with no murder charge hanging over his head.

"Now that I'm no longer thirsty or hungry — I could sleep forever," Della said wistfully.

"You can start right now," he said, his voice faintly edged. "You'll get a few hours, anyway."

He rose, walked to where the sorrel stood. He unsaddled him, picketed him in a new stand of grass. He returned to the fire a few minutes later with his blanket roll and spread it out for her.

"Yours," he said and stepped back.

She studied him for a moment. "What will you use?"

"Ground will suit me."

He didn't mention the need for keeping sharp watch throughout the night. If Toon or Duff Reemer had heard the rifle shot, they would be closing in, swiftly, quietly, and with the sole intention of killing him. He intended to be ready. He watched her crawl onto the blanket, stretch out gratefully. Her bright hair spread about her head, and the firelight, dancing upon it, set up a shimmering lake of vivid color. Looking down at her he had his first realization of how desirable and beautiful Della Stockton actually was. Another time, another place, and given different circumstances . . . He turned away.

"When will we start for that town — Frisco Springs, I think it is?"

"I'll wake you, never fear," he said bluntly.

He saw her eyes flare at the abruptness of his tone. He had not meant to be sharp, but the frustrations that had piled upon him had kindled his temper, made him unreasonable. And now pride would not allow him to apologize. He came back to the fire, added another handful of sticks to the flames. The late hours would bring a harsh chill and he should keep it going throughout the night.

He began to prowl the darkness, collecting fuel and placing it where it would be handy. Once he stood for a time gazing down at her, now in absolute repose. Her skin looked creamy in the mellow light. The sun's flush had faded and a softness had taken over. Her lips were slightly parted and her breast rose and fell gently with the rhythm of her breathing. A wisp of golden hair trailed across her forehead and touched the soil. Not conscious of his action, he bent down, lifted it and put it back into place. It was an odd thing for him to do and, thinking of it, he grinned wonderingly and walked away.

He brought his saddle and the rifle he had snatched up from Holum Reemer's side, and positioned them in the deep shadows just beyond the fan of fire glow. He made one final check of the gelding, satisfied himself the horse was resting well. He then strode to the south edge of the water hole, stood for a time studying the starlight-flooded desert. He saw nothing that aroused interest or alarm in him, and finally returned to the camp.

Near exhaustion, he sprawled out on the still warm earth, pillowing his head on his saddle. He knew he could not permit himself to sleep — only rest, and even this rankled him. They had lost far too much time. By all odds the killer on the sorrel horse was gone, escaping into the limitless frontier, leaving him with a blight he could never erase. And to his back the two men who thirsted for his blood would be gaining, closing in. He swore quietly. He would give the sorrel only four or five hours. . . . Then they would move on. . . .

That mysterious inner mechanism of men who live always within the circle of peril jarred him suddenly to wakefulness. His eyes flew open abruptly, but, schooled in the ways of danger, he did not stir, simply remained motionless in the darkness, and listened.

The fire was down to coals, glowed faintly in the night breeze. He had no way of knowing how long he had slept, of what the time might be. He guessed it was somewhere past midnight.

And he had no idea of what had awakened him.

He lay completely still, waited out the long, tense moments. Something had moved, had made sound. An animal, perhaps — or it could be a man. He could see Della. She slept the deathlike sleep of the utterly exhausted. Beyond her the darker, blurred bulk of the gelding loomed against the brush. He, too, was quiet.

Back off to his left, a stick cracked sharply. The muscles of Campion's long body grew taut. He felt the hair on his nape prickle. It was no animal, no curious coyote or lesser varmint. A man had made that noise; a man who had seen him where he lay, had taken care to double around and come up from behind.

Campion forced himself to lie motionless, to feign sleep. The sound had not been too far distant. Twelve, maybe fifteen feet at most. He calculated carefully, judging the time it would require a man to cover that space, moving slowly and cautiously. He rode out his thudding heart beats — and suddenly there was no time left.

He heard the quick step of the intruder, the dry swish of brush pushed away. Campion hurled himself to one side, felt powerful hands clutch at his body, miss their clawing purchase and go sliding off.

He bounded to his feet, wheeled to meet the attack. The shadowy figure on the ground gathered his feet under him, lunged, curses bubbling from his lips. Matt Campion did not need to see the face of the man who sought his life. The course, raspy voice was enough.

Duff Reemer.

20

Campion rocked to one side, endeavored to throw himself from the path of the charging Reemer. His foot caught against something and he went down. Reemer's full weight crashed onto him. His breath exploded in a windy blast and lights danced before his eyes as his head struck solid ground. He felt Duff's fingers clawing at his throat.

"I'll kill you!" Reemer's wild voice screamed at him. "You stoled my reward money — you run off with my woman — I'll kill you —"

A tremendous rage soared through Matt Campion. He had asked for none of this. It had no real meaning for him. It had been thrust upon him, made a crucial factor in his life — a life he was now forced to battle for. He swore feelingly, struck at Reemer with the heel of his hand. The blow caught the evil-smelling man on the bridge of the nose. Reemer howled, loosened his grasp upon Campion's throat. Matt lashed out again, this time with all the strength he could muster. He was prone, could get little leverage or force, and there was no real power in his arms.

Reemer shifted his weight and he knew he had hurt the man. He twisted under Duff's body, got partly free. Reemer struggled frantically to hold him, to keep him pinned flat, but Campion, now able to move, heaved him aside. He drove his elbow with shocking force into Reemer's kidney, and rolled free.

Campion bounded to his feet, breathing gustily. He pivoted fast, anger a yellow haze before him. He swung a balled fist, putting all he had into it. His knuckles grazed Reemer's head as he was coming off his knees. It rocked him but he did not go down. Deep, animal snarls were rumbling in Duff Reemer's throat and in the pale starlight his eyes were black pockets of hate.

"I'll kill you —"

Campion drove another stinging blow into Reemer's face, danced back before the big man's groping fingers could trap him. Duff swayed momentarily but stayed on his feet. Campion swore again, now at himself. There was no weight to his punches, no force. And he had no wind. The punishment his body had taken in the past few days and nights was showing up in depleted strength.

Reemer inched forward. He was a raving, gibbering maniac bent to one purpose — killing the man who, he fancied in his twisted mind, had wronged him. He babbled incoherently about having been robbed of both money and his woman, of being cheated out of his due. The death of his two brothers seemed to be no factor in his rage for revenge; it was only money and the red-haired girl that drove him.

It made little sense to Campion until he recognized the depth of the madness that possessed the man. But that did not lessen the danger. Dying for one reason was the same as dying for another. Matt continued to back slowly, alert for any sudden move on the part of Reemer.

He must, at all costs, keep clear of Duff's murderous hands. He realized that now, in his weakened condition, he would be no match in a test with the crazed man. His one chance was to stay away, continue to hammer at Reemer in the hope of eventually wearing him down and then driving home a telling blow.

And he must take care not to fall. That could prove fatal. He needed to get on a more even footing, out of the rocks and brush to where he could maneuver better and with greater speed. He watched Duff narrowly. The man was a chilling sight. His hair stood about his head in wild disarray, his grease-matted beard was filled with sand and dirt and bits of trash, collected when he went headlong onto the ground; his broad, yellowed teeth were bared, and his eyes, invisible in the half-light, were only dark holes in his evil face. He came on in a low crouch, arms thrust forward, fingers splayed into wicked claws.

He lunged, his movements surprisingly fast for so large a man. Matt jerked to one side, chopped a hard blow to the man's neck as he reeled by. Reemer roared, spun, lashed out blindly. The rock-hard heel of his hand caught Campion on the side of his head, sent him staggering toward the fire.

Reemer shouted in triumph. He rushed in, huge right fist raised high, poised to smash Campion. Matt dodged instinctively, without conscious thought. Reemer checked himself, whirled, and brought his foot up, aiming for Campion's groin. Matt twisted, took the brutal blow on his hip. He snatched at Reemer's booted foot, caught it, lifted upwards. Duff yelled, went crashing back into the brush.

Beyond him Campion could see Della.

She had pulled back, away from the fearful struggle. Her face was a pale, indistinct blur, frozen into immobility by the terror that held her. Farther on, back of her, the sorrel, turned nervous by the noise and confusion, milled about uncertainly.

"I'll kill you —" Reemer chanted his monotonous promise. "I'll kill you for robbin' me —"

"You damned fool!" Campion snarled in furious exasperation. "I didn't steal anything of yours!"

Reemer shouted something, struggled to get back on his feet. He seemed to have difficulty in getting his legs organized.

"Listen to me!" Campion yelled. "Listen to me! I didn't want to kill your brother. I had to — he shot at me first. And the other one — Buster. He was in the house while it was burning. I tried to get him to come out but he froze there — wouldn't move. I had no chance to go after him."

"You took my red-haired woman!" Reemer babbled idiotically. "You went and beat me out of my reward money! Ain't no man goin' to do that to me — no man! You hear? I aim to collect and take my red-haired woman —"

Della's nerves cracked at that instant. She screamed, the sound an eerie, piercing wail that split the night. Campion, startled, flung a quick glance at her. Duff Reemer's arm came up in sudden motion. The handful of sand and trash he had gathered struck Campion full in the face, momentarily blinded him. Matt staggered back, clawing at his eyes. He came up hard against a stunted juniper, tripped, went to one knee. It saved his life.

He had a vision of Reemer surging in at him, a length of wood in his hands. It came down in a blurred arc, missed only by inches. Reacting from instinct, Matt threw himself aside. Reemer lashed out with the bit of tree limb again. It grazed Campion's head. Campion rolled desperately. An arm's length away he saw the rifle, standing where he had placed it. He rolled again, snatched up the weapon. There was no time to lever the action, to be certain a bullet waited in the chamber. Duff Reemer was rushing in once more, club lifted, ready to strike, curses pouring from his lips. Matt pressed the trigger.

He saw Reemer's body jolt from the impact of the heavy-caliber bullet at such close range. Dust puffed from the man's shirt. His arms flew wide and the club sailed off into the brush as he went over backwards. He struggled to sit up, his huge head wagging back and forth grotesquely. He hung there for several breathless seconds and then collapsed.

A wild, surging fury still claimed Matt Campion. He leaped to his feet, sucking for wind in great, wrenching gasps. He took a half a dozen plunging steps forward, halted over the lifeless body of Duff Reemer. All the strain, all the bitter hate, all the nagging anxieties rushed to a single, towering head and crested in an echoing challenge.

"All right, Toon! Come on — damn you! I'm ready! Where are you, Toon?"

And then reason once again took over. He became aware of Della at his side, sobbing raggedly. He stared at her, wondered at her tears — relief for herself, horror at the death of Reemer, or because he had emerged from the fight safely?

But the simmering temper of the man kept him stiff and unyielding. "Let's get out of here," he snapped, wheeling away abruptly.

He snatched up his blanket roll, stalked toward the sorrel. The unbridled anger still burned through him and he was all raw impatience. He threw his gear onto the gelding in quick, deft motions. Finished, he spun to her.

"Wait here. Reemer's horse will be close

by. I'll get him for you to ride."

He moved off into the shadowy night. Fifty yards down he located the dead man's mount, tied to a tree. He jerked the leathers free and started back. This was one thing he could thank Reemer for; the sorrel would not have to carry double now, and they could make better time. He re-entered the clearing where Della waited. He thrust the reins at her.

"Mount up," he said, jerking Reemer's rifle from the boot and checking its magazine. It was full. He was now well armed.

She did not move, simply looked at him. "Aren't — aren't you going to bury the — the body?"

"Let him rot!" Campion snarled. "Let the coyotes and buzzards have him. He's not worth the trouble!"

"No!" she cried, the word leaping from her lips. "You can't do that — not even to him!"

"Why?" he demanded savagely. "He'd do the same if it was me — or anybody else. Deserves what he gets."

"You can't do it," Della said stubbornly. "Man came out of the caves thousands of years ago, became civilized and left all that behind — or supposedly did. In this terrible country — I'm beginning to wonder."

He was baffled by her insistence, and not a little disturbed. "It was him or me," he said, his anger cooling. "Didn't have much choice when he started using that club."

"I don't deny that — but you don't have to become an animal like him. You can do what any decent man would do."

He gave her a sudden, infuriated look. "All right. Lead the horses over to the edge of the brush and wait for me. Keep your eyes peeled for anything moving on the desert."

"Thank you, Matt," she said quietly and, taking the reins of the two horses, led them off into the darkness.

Campion walked to where Reemer lay. He grasped him by the shoulders, dragged him into a shallow gully. The ground was too hard for digging so he covered the body with rocks, leaves, sticks, anything that was loose and available. When he was finished Reemer's remains were safe from marauding animals.

Taking the rifle, he made his way to where Della and the horses awaited him.

"See anything?" he asked gruffly, halting beside her.

"Nothing," she replied.

Campion shook his head. "Toon's around here somewhere. He's got to be."

He helped her onto her saddle and

mounted the sorrel. For several moments he studied the broad, silver stillness that spread out before them, considering the best route to follow, assuming the lawman was near.

He came to a decision and led straight off into the desert. Better to get away from the shadowy brush and rocks, where a man could easily hide, as quickly as possible. On the starlit, open flats a man could see for an amazing distance. It worked both ways, he realized, but he preferred to take his chances there rather than in the darkness.

He spurred the sorrel to a slow lope. The water and grass, combined with a few hours' rest, had done wonders for the gelding. Duff Reemer's animal was not in such good condition, however. He had been run hard and it showed in his halting gait. But no matter. They couldn't be far from Frisco Springs.

21

They rode in silence across the hushed desert, turned soft now under its star-studded roof. There was a chill to the early morning hour, carried to them by a faint breeze all the way from the towering mountains of Mexico, far to the south. Now and then some night bird shuttled out from under the horse's hoofs, wings drumming heavily as it sped off into the night. Coyotes, back toward the buttes, flung their lonely, discordant complaints at the heavens, and once Campion thought he heard the faint, distant barking of a dog.

The desert was a world of breathless, dramatic beauty. With the garish, bold sun and its savage heat swallowed by the western rim, all things had changed, had taken on new form and color. The glittering sand became a smooth, misty gray carpet shot here and there by dark shadows. Rocks lost their sharpness, were only vague, blurred shapes in the night. Lowly mesquite, grease-wood, and cacti now stood proud and strong, and the humble, flat-growing ground plants, unnoticed by day, had taken on new vigor with the advent of coolness, and many now bloomed red and purple and purest yellow.

It was an altogether different world, a land turned ethereal by the gentle cloak of darkness. And through it all, oblivious to its hushed grandeur, rode Matt Campion, a man touched by violence and concerned only with the promise of death that haunted him with a relentless persistence.

He would have felt better with his heavy pistol back in its accustomed place at his hip. Its weight was an assurance, a comfort — and a guarantee. The hours during which the oiled and worn leather holster had hung empty were a time of doubt and insecurity. His symbol of independence and security had been missing and, in a world brash with danger, he had seemingly walked naked.

But he had survived.

The wonder of that stirred him. He glanced at Della Stockton — a woman, little more than a girl in fact. Alone in a vast, unfriendly land, armed only with courage, she, too, had faced the perils. And she had come through, still serene, uncomplaining, and scarcely touched by the brutality of it all.

It was a different thing, Matt Campion told himself; altogether and entirely different. Men did not war on women. They confined their killing to other men. Yet, had Duff Reemer won out, her life would have been worth less than a plugged penny. And back, before that, back in the hollow where he had come upon the Stocktons and their broken wagon, her future had indeed been bleak. Yet she had exhibited no fear. He pondered that, balancing the qualities of danger, one against the other. In the end he found no satisfactory answer, and this disturbed him.

But it in no way decreased his constant vigilance. He knew only one way to meet the threat of danger and he employed it now, riding silently along on the sorrel, his eyes whipping across the flats as he sought to trap any motion that would indicate a threat. His ears were attuned to all sounds, receiving them, recording them, separating them as to friendly or otherwise.

The rifle, Holum's rifle, lay across his lap, ready for instantaneous use. Once he saw Della place her glance upon it, upon him, as though assessing the hard, brittle wariness that rode him, and then she looked away, frowning. It did not alter his line of thought or his intentions. He had no other answer to the sure and certain knowledge that Albert Toon was somewhere nearby ready to take his life, and that his only hope of surviving was his skill with a weapon.

And use that skill he would if need be. It was not that he wished to shoot it out with the lawman. Such was far from his wishes; but not Albert Toon or any other man alive was going to prevent his finding the killer who had caused him to become a hunted man. It was a strange paradox; he would kill to prove his innocence of a murder. But that was the way of it in a land where face values were too often confused with fact. Maybe Della was right. Men were not as civilized as they assumed.

"Matt — my horse."

Della's voice broke into his sober thoughts. He glanced back without breaking the sorrel's stride. The punishment Duff Reemer had meted out to the animal was taking its toll now. But they were close to the settlement. They had to be.. They must not slow down now.

"Keep pushing him," he said. "He'll last out."

"The poor beast —"

"He'll make it," Campion snapped.

She said no more and he maintained his grim silence. Another hour wore by. The gray in the east began to brighten, slowly bloomed and became a vivid fan of color. Campion wondered about Albert Toon. The lawman should have made his move long before that moment. Why was he hanging back, holding off? Could he have been delayed, perhaps met with an accident?

He wondered if Duff Reemer had located the lawman, and immediately decided he had not. If he had, Toon would surely have been with Reemer, and they would have arrived together at the water hole. Where then was Toon? Even if they had passed each other in the darkness after the fight with Duff, the lawman would now have had time to appear in the distance. But the desert was empty. . . .

"There's the town. . . ." he heard Della say with a thankful sigh.

He brought his attention around to the double line of weather-beaten structures etched against a green background of trees and brush.

"We've made it. Now it's all over with."

He cast a sideways glance at her. She was smiling wearily and the sun, just coming over the horizon, changed her hair to gold web.

"Not yet — not for me," he murmured.

His eyes returned to the street, probed along the deserted, empty-looking structures. He sought first the livery barn — a place where a man might stable his horse.

"There's the marshal's office — over to the left," she said in a hopeful voice.

He shook his head. "My problem, not his."

His gaze was on a broad, sprawling building immediately on the opposite side. A faded sign proclaimed it as CATE'S LIVERY STABLE & FEED STORE.

"Find the hotel," he said, not looking at her. "I'll take care of my business and meet you there."

"But if you told the marshal —"

"The hotel," he said bluntly, pointedly.

He touched the gelding lightly with his heels, started him at faster pace toward the stable. At that moment a figure detached itself from the building to his left, the first in the irregular, false-fronted line. Campion drew up short. Breath eased from his lips in a soft sigh.

It was Albert Toon.

22

Campion heard Della's low, tense voice. "Is that Toon?"

"That's him," he replied quietly.

Toon was worn and beat. His mustache drooped and a thick stubble of dark beard covered his cheeks and chin. His face was beet-red from the glaring sun. His mouth was a down-curving, set line and his eyes appeared so pale as to be colorless. The blue serge vest and pants were rumpled and sweat-stained, his boots gray with dust. He had removed the celluloid collar and now there was only the narrow shirt band, closed by a small, copper button, encircling his fleshy neck.

"So," he said in a flat tone, "it iss the end of the trail for you, eh, Campion?"

Matt looked beyond the lawman into Frisco Springs' deserted street. His mind moved in a swift, orderly channel as he searched for a way out, for a means to delay

Toon and the inevitable. Fifteen minutes was all he needed; fifteen minutes in which to look for the man on the sorrel, to find proof of his existence.

"Didn't expect to see you," he drawled, stalling. "How'd you get around me?"

"The storm," Toon said. "I pass you in the storm. It wass a bad one."

"You didn't stop?"

"Yah, I stop, but after you stop. Then I ride on. I thought you were in front. Only this morning did I look back with my glasses and see you and the woman."

"This morning?" Campion echoed.

He was easing himself about slowly in the saddle, an inch at a time, trying to get set. If he could drop off the gelding, get behind the big red horse fast enough . . . Down the street beyond Toon a stocky man wearing a star had moved out of a doorway into the open, had paused and turned his glance toward them.

"How long you been here?"

"One hour, maybe a bit more," Toon said. "You will drop that rifle, Campion. There will be no more foolishness."

The town marshal had walked farther into the street and now strolled toward them, his interest aroused.

"The rifle, Campion — drop it. This time

I take no chance on you." Toon moved his ugly, short-barreled revolver threateningly.

Matt lifted the rifle slowly, let it slide to the dust.

Matt sat perfectly still, both hands raised slightly, palms down.

"Toon, I'm not asking favors, but I want to look around the town for the real killer, the man on the sorrel. He's here, or has been here. Give me fifteen minutes —"

"I give you nothing," the lawman said coldly. "I take you back to Harmony town to be hung. Or I kill you now."

"You've got to let him!" Della cried suddenly. "He can prove he's innocent!"

Toon's placid stare did not waver. "Lady, you are not mixed up in this. I saw where he met you, and you went with him. You do not know this man. He iss a killer, a bad man. The law says so."

"He didn't kill those men —"

"Get away from him, lady. Ride your horse on into the town. Do not stay close to him. This iss business of the law."

The marshal of Frisco Springs had quickened his step, came now to a halt behind Toon. He was frowning.

"Name's Antrum. What's the trouble here?"

Toon did not turn. "I am Albert Toon. I

am arresting this man for murder. I follow him two hundred miles."

Apparently the famed Mantracker had never been heard of by Antrum. "Happens this is my town. How is it you didn't look me up first?"

"No time," Albert Toon replied. "I have been here only one hour or so."

"Still should have seen me first," Antrum said, dry and dissatisfied.

Campion, seizing the opening, said, "Marshal, I'm not guilty of those murders and I came here to prove it. Man who did the killings was headed this way. I've been on his trail. He should have got here last night sometime, or maybe yesterday afternoon. Rode a big sorrel like mine. You see him?"

Antrum thought for a moment. "Nope, can't say that I did. Don't mean he couldn't have showed up, however. Was out playin' cards with a few of the boys last night. Turned in about midnight."

"All I'm asking for is a chance to look around, see if there's a sorrel stabled somewhere."

Antrum cleared his throat, spat. "Sounds reasonable to me."

Toon wagged his head stubbornly. "This iss talk, no more. This man Campion was identified as the killer. There iss a witness —"

"He lied!" Campion broke in. "Admitted it to me."

"I will need your jail, Marshal," Toon said, ignoring Matt. "I am from the United States marshal's office. I am a deputy. I will rest and start back tonight with him. It iss agreed?"

Antrum stared briefly at Toon's broad back. "Reckon it will have to be. Your badge gives you the jurisdiction —"

"No!"

It was Della. Her voice shattered the warm hush like a cracking bullwhip. She had slipped from the saddle, had seized Duff Reemer's rifle and had it leveled at the two lawmen.

"You're going to give him a chance to prove his innocence," she said firmly. Her eyes were a bright, flashing blue and her hair a flame in the sunlight. "It won't hurt you to let him look — and he has the right to prove he's telling the truth."

This was a new Della — a different Della, one who now recognized the value of force. Campion grinned tightly at her determination. The two lawmen shifted nervously. Toon found his voice.

"Now, lady, you can't —"

"I can — and I am," she said. "You men! What's the matter with you? How can you always be so sure you're right?"

"Put down that gun, lady," Toon said, his usual stolid composure showing signs of distress. "This man iss a killer. The law says so."

"The law says so! Can't the law be wrong — is it always so right?"

"You hadn't ought to mix yourself up in this," Antrum said. "May be some things you don't know —"

"Matt!" Della suddenly cried. "The stable there — the side door! A man on a horse like yours!"

Campion's attention swiveled to the livery barn. He caught a glimpse of a rider just pulling away from the building, walking his mount fast toward an alleyway a dozen yards distant.

"Hold up — you!" Campion yelled.

The rider flung a hurried glance over his shoulder. His face was taut, strained — and vaguely familiar.

"Hendrick!"

The name was an explosive burst from Albert Toon's lips. "Hendrick — halt!"

Campion stared. Hendrick . . . Henry . . . Henry Toon. It wasn't possible — yet there he was. The resemblance to his brother was remarkable.

The man on the sorrel whirled. Metal glinted in his hand. He fired. The bullet dug into the sand at the lawman's feet, sent up a spurt of powdery dust. Toon lurched to one side, his own gun blasting through the echoes of the first shot. Henry Toon jolted, stiffened. He buckled, fell heavily to the ground, and the sorrel shied off toward the stable.

For the space of a long breath no one moved, and then Albert Toon, smoking pistol still in his hand, started for the fallen man. Campion, off his horse and with Della at his shoulder, followed. Antrum, backed now by a score of rapidly assembling citizens, also fell in behind the lawman.

They halted beside the stricken rider, formed a circle around him. Albert Toon stood for a few moments gazing down, then he knelt.

"Hendrick, it iss me, Albert."

Henry Toon opened his eyes. He looked up into the marshal's face, a faint, twisted smile on his lips.

"I fooled you, Albert. I fooled them all. . . . And I almost got away with it. . . ."

"Yah, Hendrick — almost. Who wass the man you killed and put in the buggy — in your place? Who wass he, Hendrick?"

Henry Toon's face drew into sly, ugly corners. "You are the big hero, Albert. You are the big lawman — you find out," he said, and closed his eyes.

Toon did not move for another full minute. Then his pudgy hands reached out, dug inside the dead man's shirt. He fumbled for a bit and then drew forth a money belt thick with currency and coins. Without looking around he handed it to Antrum.

"You will please count the money, Marshal. There will be near forty-five hundred dollars."

Campion felt Della's fingers on his arm. "I don't understand all this. Who —"

Comprehension had come quickly to Matt. He explained it now to the girl. Henry Toon had planned a clever crime. He had killed the bank clerk and some luckless drifter who happened to be handy. He had then changed clothes with the drifter, made it appear it was he himself who had been murdered. Using a shotgun on the man's head and setting fire to the buggy in which the two bodies had been placed insured the identification. He had then ridden north with the money, believing he had pulled a perfect job. It was only the fact the drifter's horse had been a sorrel that had tripped him up.

Campion shifted his glance to Albert Toon. The old lawman's face was blank but he was remembering something — something dark and bitter that was not to his liking. It was there in his eyes.

"Reckon you're through with me," Matt said, unable to keep the slight edge from his voice.

Toon nodded slowly. "Yah, yah, I am. And I am sorry, Campion."

Matt felt Della bristle against him. "Sorry!" she exclaimed. "You hound him for days and nights, you try your best to kill him — and all you can say is that you're sorry! What if that man there — your brother — hadn't been here? What if he had stayed hidden, hadn't tried to run?"

Toon did not meet her blazing eyes. "I am sorry, lady. No more can I say."

Campion placed his arm about Della's shoulders, drew her about. "It's all right. It's all over now."

"But you could have been hanged — killed. . . ."

"Way it goes sometimes. Best thing to do is forget it." He looked off down the street. "Hotel over there. And a café. What say we get cleaned up and have a good meal?"

She looked at him closely. "You sound different. Not so grim, so hard."

He rubbed at the stubble on his chin. "Now that it's all done with, I feel different. And if I was a mite sharp with you back there on the trail, I'm sorry."

"Sorry — I could hate that word."

"Poor pay I know, but like Toon, it's the best I can do — and I'm trying to set things right with you."

"Why bother?" she murmured. "I'll soon be gone, out of your life, out of your way."

"Just what I'm getting at. Hoped maybe I could talk you into becoming a rancher's wife, not leave at all. I'm going to buy a place —"

She whirled to him, eyes bright, hair shining in the sun like burnished gold. "You know the answer to that, Matt Campion!"

ABOUT THE AUTHOR

Ray Hogan is an author who has inspired a loyal following over the years since he published his first Western novel *Ex-marshal* in 1956. Hogan was born in Willow Springs, Missouri, where his father was town marshal. At five the Hogan family moved to Albuquerque where Ray Hogan still lives in the foothills of the Sandia and Manzano mountains. His father was on the Albuquerque police force and, in later years, owned the Overland Hotel. It was while listening to his father and other old-timers tell tales from the past that Ray was inspired to recast these tales in fiction. From the beginning he did exhaustive research into the history and the people of the Old West and the walls of his study are lined with various firearms, spurs, pictures, books, and memorabilia, about all of which he can talk in dramatic detail. Among his most popular works are the series of books about Shawn Starbuck, a searcher in a quest for a lost brother, who has a clear sense of right and wrong and who is willing to stand up and be counted when it is a question of fairness or justice. His other major series is about lawman John Rye whose reputation has earned him the sobriquet 'The Doomsday Marshal'. 'I've attempted to capture the courage and bravery of those men and women that lived out West and the dangers and problems they had to overcome,' Hogan once remarked. If his lawmen protagonists seem sometimes larger than life, it is because they are men of integrity, heroes who through grit of character and common sense are able to overcome the obstacles they encounter despite often overwhelming odds. This same grit of character can also be found in Hogan's heroines and, in *The Vengeance of Fortuna West,* Hogan wrote a gripping and totally believable account of a woman who takes up the badge and tracks the men who killed her lawman husband by ambush. No less intriguing in her way is Nellie Dupray, convicted of rustling in *The Glory Trail.* Above all, what is most impressive about Hogan's Western novels is the consistent quality with which each is crafted, the compelling depth of his characters, and his ability to juxtapose the complexities of human conflict into narratives always as intensely interesting as they are emotionally involving.

JB

WR